MW00917948

Hired Bride

Beaufort Brides, Book 1

NOELLE ADAMS

ONE

Deanna Beaufort's family line could be traced back almost three hundred years.

One of the Beauforts fought against the British in the Siege of Savannah in 1778 and another defended the city against the Northerners in 1864. Deanna's grandmother had told her stories about all the great Beauforts of the past since the time she was three years old. She knew them all by heart. They were as familiar to her as her neighbors.

The old Beaufort house in Savannah had been built in the early nineteenth century and had never been out of the family's possession. When they'd had money, the house was a point of pride. Now, however, it was just a money pit, and it had been crumbling down around Deanna's head for as long as she could remember.

At the moment, it was the grand staircase that was in danger of collapsing beneath their feet. Deanna and her youngest sister, Kelly, were on their hands and knees, trying to nail down the loose planks before someone tripped on one and cracked open their skull.

"This is ridiculous," Kelly said, pushing one of her long braids back behind her shoulder and her glasses back up her nose. "Tacking some wood down isn't going to do any good. The whole staircase needs to be rebuilt."

Deanna sat up, sighing as she looked up at the dilapidated stairs. She used to slide down the balustrade when she was a girl, but she wouldn't dare put any weight on it now. She loved the old house, and it hurt her almost physically to see it in such bad shape. "I know. But unless you're prepared to do it yourself, then it's not going to get done. It will take us five years to save up enough money to pay for that kind of work."

"I know. If you'd let me get a job, I could—"

"No," Deanna said sharply. "You're finishing college first. We've had this discussion before."

Their parents had died when they were kids, and they'd been raised by their grandmother ever since. The life insurance had run out several years ago since their grandmother wasn't exactly into frugal living, so money had been tight for a while. Deanna worked as a receptionist in a marketing company—without a college degree, that was the best she could do—and their middle sister, Rose, worked as a nanny for a family who was presently summering in London. But the sisters had decided a long time ago that Kelly would get through college since she was the most academically minded of the three.

If their grandmother had her wish, all three would be married to wealthy men by now, but so far that hadn't happened. Deanna was twenty-six, and she hadn't had a serious boyfriend in four years. She was pretty sure that her eccentric, intimidating grandmother scared away any guy who might otherwise be interested, but she didn't dare say that out loud.

Her grandmother loved her and had raised them when they'd had absolutely no one else. So what if she was obsessed with their family history—so much so that it caused her to act irrationally a lot of the time? Deanna wasn't going to give up on her.

Since she'd been eleven and her parents' had died in the car accident, she'd worked desperately to hold her family together, often a losing battle as they always seemed on the verge of disaster.

"*What* are you doing?" The sharp voice came from behind them and startled Deanna so much she jerked.

She turned to see her grandmother, a small woman with a rigid posture who always wore a black dress and a tight bun. "We're working on these loose boards. I almost fell down the steps earlier because I tripped on one."

"Well, you can do it later. We need to leave for the ball in thirty minutes."

The "ball" was a black-tie party at the country club for which her grandmother refused to give up her membership. Three or four times a year, Deanna was hauled to one of the parties and foisted on any available bachelor who happened to be present.

She'd known what was coming this evening, but she'd been hoping that pretending it didn't exist might make it go away.

That particular strategy never worked, but she kept trying.

"I was thinking that maybe I wouldn't go to—"

"You must," her grandmother interrupted.

"But I've met all the available men who ever attend. None of them are interested in me. It's not like I'm going to find my future husband there, so it feels like a waste of—"

"It is not a waste. There might be someone new. And Morris Alfred Theobald III might attend."

Her grandmother's latest scheme was to match her up with Morris, a short, balding, pompous ass who was always referred to by his full name. Deanna couldn't stand him, and

3

she had spent most of the last social function trying to avoid his groping hands.

He was rich though, so her grandmother thought he'd be a good match.

"Now go get ready," her grandmother said. "Wear the green dress."

Deanna sighed and stood up, giving Kelly a wry look. Over and over again, she daydreamed about defying her grandmother and just saying no. It was a ridiculous, anachronistic idea anyway—finding a rich husband to restore the family fortune. But every time she was on the verge of rebelling, she would see something that looked like desperation in her grandmother's eyes.

The family meant everything to her grandmother. And in her worldview, the only way to save the family was to marry a man who could bring in the money they needed. Deanna could hardly expect the old woman to have kept up with the times. If the choice was giving up an evening to go to a party or breaking her grandmother's heart, Deanna would always choose giving up the evening.

It was a small enough thing, after all. She didn't want to hurt her grandmother.

"Kelly," her grandmother said, "The Pride needs to be dusted."

Deanna and Kelly looked at each other. "The Pride" was a collection of Mrs. Beaufort's dead Siamese cats, all professionally stuffed by a taxidermist to preserve them. They were prominently displayed in the parlor, along with a host of other family treasure including china and costumes from their Beaufort forebears.

In high school, Deanna had never dared invite friends inside the house since they invariably laughed at the museum she lived in. Now she found it rather endearing. In a world that cared more about the next big thing, she thought it was meaningful that her grandmother wanted to remember good things from the past.

Kelly nodded. She was just nineteen, but she'd always been oddly mature and sensible. "I'll dust them this evening when y'all leave. Deanna might need my help getting dressed."

Deanna didn't need any help—certainly not from Kelly, whose idea of fashion was a baggy T-shirt and braids—but she was glad for the company as she went upstairs to get dressed. She showered quickly and came back into her room to find her sister was trying to smooth out a few wrinkles on the silvery-green dress that Rose, who was an excellent seamstress, had made for her last year.

A few minutes later, Kelly was eying her sister moodily as Deanna worked on her long brown hair.

"What's the matter?" Deanna asked, noticing her sister's uncharacteristically sober expression.

"Nothing. Just one day you're going to have to say no to her."

Deanna knew immediately who the "her" referred to. "I say no to her plenty."

"Yeah, on little things that don't mean anything. But you won't say no to her on big things."

Deanna stiffened her shoulders. She'd done her makeup, so the face looking at her in the mirror was fresh and pretty, with familiar large light gray-green eyes and full lips. Around her neck was a lovely beaded necklace that she'd made herself. In her little spare time, she loved working with beads. "Yes, I will. Going to a party isn't a big deal. There's no sense in making a stand over something so little. If it's important, I'll say no to her. For instance, I'll never date Morris Alfred Theobald III, even if she wants me to."

"Maybe. But sometimes I wonder. You should be living on your own now, using your salary to build a life for yourself instead of trying to take care of all of us. You don't have a life at all because you're trapped by all of us and our weirdness."

"I am not trapped," Deanna said sharply, surprised and worried by the turn of the conversation. Kelly was so self-possessed that it was sometimes difficult to know what was going on in her mind. "I love you all. I live here and help with money because I choose to, because it makes me happy. I'd be miserable if I just up and left you in the lurch."

"I know you'd feel guilty, but the point is, you shouldn't have to feel guilty for living your own life. It's like you're always trying to hold everything together for us, and you shouldn't have to do that."

"Kelly, stop. *This* is my life. I'm not some sort of sacrificial lamb for the family. I like my job, and I like living here, and I love all of you, and it's not the end of the world to go to a few parties. You'd do the same thing."

"I'd be terrible at a party. Grandmama would never take me. I'd humiliate her."

This was true. Kelly had always been a tomboy growing up, and she still had absolutely no social graces. Their grandmother would never try to marry her off until she had no other choice. Since Rose was a live-in nanny, she wasn't in the position of being pushed onto the marriage mart.

No, it was only Deanna who got that joy—at least for the time being.

Sometimes it was embarrassing. She knew that people laughed at her grandmother and talked about her obvious ambition to get rich husbands for her granddaughters.

She shook the thought away. She'd lived with it for a long time, and it didn't change the most important things.

She loved her family, and she would do anything she could to make them happy and take care of them.

If that meant going to a fancy party and being thrown at any eligible men who happened to be present, then she could live with that.

~

The party was exactly as Deanna had expected.

It was mostly the same crowd as always attended these functions, and she greeted her friends and acquaintances with conversations that felt like they'd been replayed dozens of times before.

At least Morris Alfred Theobald III wasn't present.

She only saw a few people she didn't know. One of them was a very attractive man she had trouble keeping her eyes off of. He looked to be in his thirties, and he was taller than anyone else in the room, with an impressive build, classically handsome features, and a kind of lurking charisma that seemed to attract people like a magnet. He was the only man not wearing a tuxedo.

She didn't know who he was, but he appeared to have a date—Gina Fenton—so she had to assume he wasn't available.

If he was, her grandmother would find out soon enough and drag her over to meet him.

Deanna was sneaking another look at the good-looking, dark-haired man when a voice from behind her surprised her. "Deanna, how lovely you look tonight."

She turned to see a matronly middle-aged woman she recognized. "Mrs. Damon," she said with a smile. "Thank you. How are you?"

Lucy Damon was as much a fixture at these parties as her grandmother was, and Deanna had known her most of her life. The Damons were rich and successful, with their hotels and restaurants all over the world. Deanna had dated Lucy's son, Benjamin, in high school, and she knew her grandmother was crushed that she hadn't managed to snare him.

"I'm doing very well. Benjamin and Mandy are getting married. Did you hear about that?"

"No, I didn't!" Deanna smiled at the news. "Congratulations. You must be thrilled. When is the wedding?"

"In three months. They're going to get married here in Savannah. I hope you'll be able to attend."

"I wouldn't miss it." Deanna was still smiling with pleasure at hearing how well Ben and Mandy were doing—she'd only met Mandy briefly, but she'd immediately liked the sweet, pretty young woman. Then her eyes drifted over to the handsome man she didn't know again.

He happened to be looking in her direction too, so their eyes met across the room.

It was one of those strange moments that feel intense for no good reason. Flustered, Deanna turned back to Lucy Damon.

Lucy had turned to see who had distracted her. "Oh, do you know Mitchell Graves?"

"No," Deanna said hurriedly, before the name clicked. "Oh, I've heard of him, of course, but I've never met him. He owns the Claremont, right? Is that him?"

"Yes, that's him. He's been expanding his business. That's why he's with Gina Fenton tonight. Something about that restaurant the Fentons own. And I believe he's reached out to Cyrus, although I never heard how that turned out." Lucy's brother was Cyrus Damon, billionaire and CEO of Damon Enterprises, a man just as eccentric in his own way as Deanna's grandmother. "I'm not sure why Mitchell is here tonight though. He doesn't like these traditional get-togethers. He's…"

When she trailed off, Deanna was immediately curious. "He's what?"

"He's very *modern* in his behavior," Lucy said discreetly. "He's an excellent businessman, according to my brother, but his behavior…" She cleared her throat.

"He doesn't behave well?" Deanna tried to remember what she'd heard about the man. Most of it was connected to the Claremont Hotel, which had gradually become the most prestigious hotel in the city. She also thought she remembered his name being associated with a few different women, but certainly nothing so scandalous it dominated the local gossip.

Lucy continued, "I understand he doesn't believe in traditions—including marriage. As you might expect, this has led to some ruffled feathers in Savannah. Evidently, he does love his mother though, so at least he has that going for him."

"Oh." Deanna tried to hide a smile as she glanced back at him. That was probably why he was—quite inappropriately—wearing a business suit to the party. A man who didn't believe in much-loved and well-established traditions would be anathema to a certain section of Savannah. She had to admire the brazenness, particularly since he owned a hotel that was founded on many of those traditions.

Mitchell was talking to Gina Fenton, but his eyes shifted back casually to where Deanna stood. She knew he saw her looking at him, and she glanced away immediately.

No sense in being interested in that direction. If he didn't believe in marriage, he obviously wasn't a good option for her, and a man like that would never put up with her grandmother.

Deanna wouldn't even want him.

She wasn't as consumed by the past and their lineage as her grandmother was—not even close. But it was part of who she was. And she wouldn't want to date a man who treated things that were important to her like they were nothing.

～

When her grandmother came over a few minutes later and took her arm in a steely grip, Deanna knew she was going to be bullied into an introduction.

Her grandmother only acted like this when she was on a mission, which usually meant she'd found a new eligible man.

"I was talking to Mrs. Damon," Deanna began, knowing the objection was useless, even as she said it.

"She will understand." She was heading toward the far side of the room, and Deanna could see who was standing directly in their path.

Mitchell Graves.

"Grandmama," Deanna said in a low voice, feeling a flush rising in her cheeks. "There's no sense in introducing me to—"

"He is single."

"I know, but he isn't... I mean, he won't..."

"He comes from no family, but he is rich. Talk to him. Maybe you'll like him."

Deanna almost groaned. She'd been through this many times before, and she was usually confronted with either sympathy, amusement, or faint disgust, depending on the character of the man in question.

Deanna wasn't sure what Mitchell Graves' character would be, but she somehow knew he wouldn't appreciate being seen as a potential tool for restoring the fortunes of a failing Savannah family.

"Mr. Graves," her grandmother said, her sharp voice breaking into the conversation between Mitchell and George Fenton without any warning at all. "This is my granddaughter, Deanna. You should meet her."

Deanna's cheeks were burning hotly now. She was used to her grandmother's blunt habits and brazen fortune hunting, but she could very clearly see herself through

Mitchell's eyes. He would think they were nothing but a source of contempt and mockery.

She hated feeling that way—about herself and about her grandmother.

"Grandmama," she murmured, shooting an apologetic look at the men. "We're interrupting."

"It's no problem at all," George Fenton said with a smile. He was Gina's brother—a polite middle-aged man whom Deanna had met a few times. "We shouldn't have been discussing business at a party anyway. Good to see you again, Mrs. Beaufort, Miss Deanna."

Mitchell had lifted his dark eyebrows and was studying her grandmother as if she were a strange specimen under a microscope. Then he turned his eyes to her with a look of cool amusement. "It's nice to meet you, Miss Deanna." He pronounced the last words with an emphasis that she immediately understood as mockery.

Her shoulders stiffened. She might be embarrassed by her grandmother's behavior herself, but that didn't give this man any reason to look down on them that way. "It's nice to meet you too. Sorry for the interruption," she said with as much composure as she could muster. "We'll let you get back to your conversation."

She turned to leave, resenting the hell out of Mitchell's arrogantly amused expression.

"You will stay here," her grandmother said firmly, giving her the look the sisters had always called her "evil eye"—the one that allowed no dispute. "There is no interruption."

Deanna was about to object, partly because she wanted to sink into the ground to get away from this conversation and partly because she had no interest in talking to this man who seemed to become more of an ass as the moments passed.

But her objection would upset her grandmother. She would act angry but would actually be hurt. Then Deanna would feel guilty. Then her grandmother would sulk for a few days, and the whole household would be thrown out of whack.

It just wasn't worth it. She could talk to Mitchell for a couple of minutes and not risk anyone being hurt. So she sighed and turned back.

"I will let you get acquainted," her grandmother said with a nod of satisfaction before she turned and walked away.

Mitchell's expression changed from amusement to an acute observation that looked almost disdainful. As if he was judging her. As if he thought she was weak or spineless or silly. As if he knew her at all.

She liked this man even less now than she had the moment before.

"So, what brings you here tonight?" she asked since she had to say something.

"Business," he said, his eyes drifting around the well-dressed crowd. "This ridiculous, outdated ritual isn't exactly my scene."

"Yeah, I wouldn't have thought it was." Her tone might have been a little cool, but everything in his look and tone seemed to be judging her, judging *them*, and she didn't appreciate it.

"How old are you?" he asked, his eyes landing on her face again.

She stiffened. "What kind of question is that?"

"It's a simple enough question. I don't believe in standing on ceremony, and I wanted to know."

"Why do you want to know?"

"Because you look like you're too old to still be under your grandmother's control."

She gasped in indignation. "I'm not under my grandmother's control."

The corner of his mouth twitched. "Is that the story you're going with?"

He was still ludicrously handsome, even as she wanted to scratch the skin off his face. She snapped her mouth closed to keep herself from telling him exactly what she thought of him. Instead, she turned on her heel to walk away from him.

She was sorry if it would disappoint her grandmother, but there was no way in hell she was going to spend any more time with this jackass.

Her grandmother's dreams of a rich marriage weren't going to be fulfilled with Mitchell Graves. That was for sure.

~

Mitchell Graves hated parties like this. A bunch of nostalgic idiots trying to recreate a romanticized past that had never existed.

He wouldn't have come at all, except he needed to talk to the Fentons about a business deal he really wanted to happen.

The Fentons owned the Darlington Café, and Mitchell was determined to buy them out. For the first time in years, they were considering getting out of the business, so he thought they'd very likely accept a reasonable offer as long as they liked and trusted Mitchell.

Since they believed in these throwback parties, Mitchell had to go. And he had to play nice, even though George's affability was grating on him and Gina kept flirting with him.

Mitchell was certainly not opposed to using sex when it served his purpose, but he wasn't at all attracted to Gina Fenton, and having sex with her would almost certainly come back to bite him in the ass.

So aside from the one brief encounter with Deanna Beaufort, he wasn't having a very good night.

Deanna was absolutely gorgeous—small and curvy with thick dark hair and those mesmerizing green eyes. There was a spirit that seemed trapped inside her quiet, restrained persona as if she was someone else, someone she couldn't let the rest of the world see. He could sense that in her—a kind of passion that appealed to him—even as he tried not to laugh at her grandmother's shameless attempts to pair her off with a rich man.

Mitchell didn't believe in marriage, and that wasn't going to change. It was another of those stupid things people did because they thought they had to. So he could laugh privately at the absurdity without feeling much threat.

He enjoyed it even more when Deanna obviously got angry with him and did her best to hide it.

He'd like to get to know her better, but the Darlington Café was more important.

Things had always come easily to Mitchell. He'd done well at school and in sports and in debate without even trying. He'd sailed through college and grad school, earning an MBA without breaking a sweat. He'd convinced some investors to help him buy out a dying hotel in historic Savannah since he was sure he could turn the place around.

It hadn't taken much effort on his part, but it had worked. The Claremont was now more successful than he could have imagined, and he wasn't even thirty-five years old yet.

Life was easy. Women were easy. There wasn't much sense in taking things seriously. That was one of the reasons he was so intrigued by Deanna, who seemed to take everything seriously.

He didn't have time for her tonight though. He had George Fenton squarely on his side, which meant he just had to convince Gina.

He needed to play it exactly right. She'd obviously been interested in him from the first time they met, but she was much more open about it tonight than she'd been before. If he flirted with her, she would keep coming on to him, and then things would get sticky. But if he held her at arm's length, she might get her pride hurt, and she could block the deal merely out of spite.

Mitchell was still trying to figure out the best strategy when he found her talking to her brother.

She smiled as he approached, something intimate in her expression that was troubling and entirely inappropriate, as if she was sure he would fold to her advances.

Maybe she thought he was a business whore—willing to sleep his way into the deal.

He had sex a lot. None of it serious. But the only times he had sex with a business partner or associate was when he genuinely wanted to.

He didn't want to sleep with Gina. She wasn't unattractive, but she gave him unpleasant vibes.

"Get me a drink, Mitchell?" she asked, taking his arm possessively.

"Sure." He smiled—his normal easy, charismatic smile, but his mind was working fast. He had to figure out a way out of this bind, how to reject her without offending her.

He wanted the Darlington Café. He wanted it so much he could feel it in his chest. He wasn't going to blow the deal over something so trivial.

Instead of heading for the bar, Gina pulled him into a side room off the main ballroom. Before he could react, she had him pressed up to a wall and was rubbing her body against him.

This was terrible. She was shameless, and she evidently thought he wouldn't object since he wanted the restaurant so much.

"Gina, wait," he said, trying not to sound trapped, although he was starting to feel that way.

"Why do we have to wait?" She was pressing kisses on his jaw and around his mouth.

He managed to hold her back without tightening his grip. Any moment, she was going to get mad and the whole deal would be blown. "Because I can't... I can't do this."

"Why not?"

He couldn't say he didn't want her. It might be true, but it would hopelessly offend her. "Because I'm... I'm not available."

That would work. That would be a good excuse. If he was already with someone, then he couldn't be with her and it wouldn't be personal at all.

17

Perfect.

"You're not with someone else. I would have heard." She ran her hand down his chest and abdomen until it almost reached his groin.

Mitchell really didn't want this woman to touch him there. "We're keeping it quiet to avoid gossip, but I'm already with someone else."

"Unless you're engaged…"

"I am engaged." Why the hell not? If he could have a fictional girlfriend, then he could have a fictional fiancée. That would make for an even better excuse, and it might be the only way out of this tangle.

Gina gasped audibly and stepped back. "I thought you didn't believe in marriage."

"I don't." Mitchell rubbed his face, thinking as quickly as he could. This was turning complicated, but he couldn't take it back without sacrificing the Darlington Café. "But I fell in love. What can I say? Maybe I'm predictable after all. I'm sorry if it led to any misunderstandings. But you'll understand if I can't…"

He trailed off, hoping this would be enough. He told lies when he needed to—if it was the best way to achieve his objective. It was all part of business, and this would definitely count.

"I guess so. I wish I'd known." She was starting to look a little embarrassed, which was good, but there was still a spark of suspicion in her eyes, as if she didn't quite believe him. "Who are you engaged to?"

Now he was really trapped. He'd have to make up someone from a different state, but then there would be a whole backstory he'd have to concoct to make it believable since he wasn't out of town enough for a long-distance relationship.

Maybe she could be a recluse who never left home.

Maybe she could be dying and the story could be a tragic love affair.

Maybe she could have an abusive father.

Before he could come up with a believable story, the door of the room opened and Mrs. Beaufort walked in with Deanna trailing behind.

"Grandmama," Deanna was saying, looking frustrated and tired and still incredibly pretty. "I don't need to freshen—" She broke off when she saw the room was occupied. "Oh, sorry." Her eyes slid from Mitchell to Gina and back again.

Mitchell suddenly had a brainstorm. The perfect solution to the knot he'd bound himself in. There was always an easy answer. He just had to wait until it appeared.

He turned to Gina. "This is her," he said, giving Deanna a broad smile. "This is my fiancée. Deanna Beaufort."

Deanna's big eyes got even bigger as she stared at him speechlessly.

But Mrs. Beaufort, that savvy, ambitious old lady, evidently had a mind that worked like a machine. She straightened up, a look of recognition washing over her face, and she said, "Yes, my granddaughter is engaged to Mr. Graves. We weren't planning to announce it yet, however."

"Grandmama," Deanna breathed, staring numbly at her grandmother. She was obviously too stunned to keep up.

But Mitchell had taken his measure of her in the brief conversation they'd had before, and he was sure she wasn't going to object. She obviously did anything for her grandmother, no matter how little she wanted to do it.

He could use it. It was what he did. Take a quick assessment of other people and use it for his advantage. "I know we weren't announcing it yet, but I felt like I needed to tell Ms. Fenton." He turned back to Gina. "I'm very sorry. I hope you'll understand."

"Of course." Gina didn't look offended now. She looked surprised and curious and almost maliciously intrigued. "When will you get married?"

"We haven't set the date yet," Mrs. Beaufort said, obviously thinking as quickly as Mitchell was. "We're trying to avoid a lot of gossip. You know how people are. But we are all very pleased with the match."

Mitchell had no doubts that Mrs. Beaufort was pleased. She wouldn't hesitate to use this to her advantage as well. And Mitchell was pleased to have gotten himself out of his bind without losing the sale of the Darlington Café.

But one look at Deanna's face made it clear she wasn't pleased. She appeared to still be in shock, but pretty soon it would catch up to her, and she would have a few things to say about being trapped in a pseudo engagement with him.

Mitchell would deal with it then though. He wasn't particularly worried.

He'd learned a long time ago that life could always be easy if you were smart enough to make it work for you.

TWO

"You have got to be out of your mind!"

His sister's voice reverberated through the speakers in Mitchell's car, louder than normal because she was clearly so shocked.

"Calm down," he said. "It isn't that big a deal."

"Not a big deal!" Brie was twenty-six—eight years younger than him—and they'd never been close until the past couple of years, when she'd moved back to Savannah as an adult. She'd gone to art school, specializing in stained glass work, and she was finishing up a job helping to restore an old church in the city. She was usually easygoing, so it took Mitchell aback that she was so outraged by this idea, even though he probably should have expected it.

"Of course it's a big deal! You're thinking about getting married just to get the Darlington. It's absolutely insane."

"It's not like it would be a permanent marriage. Just six months or something—long enough for the deal to go through. Then we can have an amicable divorce and move on. It will be more like a business partnership. Nothing earth-shattering about that."

"But *marriage*? What would you do with a wife? You can't even manage to get a serious girlfriend."

"Thanks a lot."

"You know what I mean. Commitment is not one of your strengths. I'm serious. You're actually planning to be a husband for six months."

"Just on paper."

There was silence on the other end of the call as Brie obviously tried to process all this. "What the hell kind of girl agreed to this wacky plan?"

"Deanna Beaufort. Have you ever met her?"

"I don't think so. Does she have some kind of crazy grandma?"

"Yes, that's her."

"I've heard the grandma has all her dead lovers stuffed and kept in a gallery in their decrepit old house."

Mitchell gave a huff of amusement. "That's nonsense. The grandmother is definitely out of touch with reality, but that's working in my favor. She's desperate to marry Deanna off to a rich man, so she jumped at this chance. It's going to work out well for both of us."

"But what about poor Deanna? She actually wants to marry you?"

"I don't think so, but she seems pretty spineless and will do whatever her grandmother wants."

"So she's being taken advantage of here? That's just great."

He cleared his throat, getting a little annoyed at how his sister was blowing it out of proportion. "She's not being sold off to the highest bidder. It's a business deal. It's just six months of her time, and they'll get to restore that monster of a house. The terms of the contract will be perfectly fair, and you don't think I'm going to be cruel to her or anything, do you?"

"Not intentionally, no."

"What is that supposed to mean?" He was starting to get offended now.

"It means you're not going to do anything to hurt her on purpose, but she may get hurt anyway. A marriage is different than a handshake, you know."

"It doesn't have to be. It's all just on paper, I've told you before."

"So you're not going to even live together."

He hesitated. "No, we'll have to, or Gina won't believe it's for real. We'll keep up appearances, but that's it. Her lifestyle with me will be more comfortable than the one she has now. What the hell will she have to complain about?"

"And what if she wants more than being treated as some sort of paid escort?"

He made a growly sound in his throat. "She's not going to want more. I don't even think she likes me, if her expression is anything to go on."

"Oh, this just gets better and better."

"Would you stop?" His tone was a little sharp since he was running out of patience. "It's just six months. I'll fix her up a room in my place exactly as she wants it. She'll only be obligated to be seen with me socially a limited amount. We don't have to interact otherwise. It will be fine."

"And she'll agree to all this?"

"We'll work it all out in a contract. No one will be taken advantage of. What kind of man do you think I am?"

Brie didn't answer right away, and when she did her tone was reluctant. "I think you're a man who's used to always getting what he wants without trying too hard. This feels like a shortcut to me, and I don't think it's a good idea. Someone is going to get hurt."

"No one is going to get hurt."

"I don't think the restaurant is worth all this."

Mitchell felt a chill run through him. "It is. You know it is."

"I know it means something to Mom, but she would never want you to—"

"She's never going to know what I did to make this happen. Promise me you won't tell her."

"Mitchell—"

"Promise me."

Brie sighed audibly. "I promise I won't tell her. But she wouldn't want this."

"I swore we'd get the restaurant back before she dies, and I'll do whatever I need to do to make it happen. This marriage is nothing compared to that."

Brie sighed. "I hope you still think so six months from now."

Mitchell bit back a sharp response since Brie always liked to have the last word. Having the last word never mattered much to him. It was easier to just let other people have it when they got like this since it didn't make any difference to reality.

No matter what his sister said or thought, this marriage wasn't a big deal. Everything would be fine.

"When do you see her again?" Brie asked in a different tone when he hadn't replied.

"I'm heading over to their house right now, just to work out some basic stuff. Then my lawyers can get on with drawing up the contract."

In the silence, it felt like Brie was shaking her head, but Mitchell managed to ignore it.

He'd always been good with people. And he wouldn't have any trouble dealing with an eccentric, fortune-hunting old woman and a compliant young woman.

~

"I can't understand how this stupid room collects so much dust," Kelly grumbled, running a disposable duster over the surface of an antique console table in their parlor on which were displayed about fifteen clocks from different eras of the family history. The parlor was the only room in the whole house that had nice furniture and freshly polished trim, so it was always the room used to see company. "Didn't we just dust it yesterday?"

Deanna shook her head, on her hands and knees, picking up the leaves that had been shed by the potted plant in one corner. "No. I think it was Wednesday, when Reverend Wilson came over."

She stood up, brushing off her cotton skirt, and went to straighten up the nineteenth-century dresses that were hanging on a display rack against one wall. "I guess it looks okay in here. The asshole is going to look down at us anyway, so it doesn't really matter. Just close the curtains over the Pride. He doesn't need to see them, for sure."

Kelly reached over to pull the cord that drew thick velvet curtains across the long shelf on which the stuffed cats were displayed.

Deanna could just imagine Mitchell's face if he saw the Pride in all their faded, creepy glory.

"Is everything prepared?" her grandmother said, striding into the room unexpectedly with a frown, wearing her best day dress—which was black and almost exactly like her others except in a more expensive fabric.

"Yes. We straightened up. I don't think it matters much though. He needs something from us, so we have the advantage here. Who cares if there's dust on the furniture or not?"

"All of it matters. This could change our entire fortune. You will be agreeable, won't you?"

Deanna let out a breath. "I'll try. But I'm only going to agree to reasonable terms."

"Naturally."

There was no naturally about it. There was nothing even remotely natural about this situation. But somehow Deanna had known something like this would happen eventually, and this was actually better than some of the nightmare marriages she'd imagined her grandmother engineering for her.

Mitchell only needed this to happen for a very limited amount of time. Then they could go their separate ways. And she was pretty sure he would leave her alone for most of their marriage, which certainly wouldn't have been the case with someone like Morris Alfred Theobald III.

She would absolutely have to say no to a marriage with Morris and completely betray her grandmother in the process.

But this would be better. This might be doable. This might be a way of remaining loyal to her grandmother without completely ruining her life. It would be more like a business arrangement than anything else.

After all, it would only last six or eight months. How bad could something like that be?

The deep resonance of the front doorbell startled her out of the reflections.

He was here. She felt a little jump in her heart.

Her grandmother went to answer the door, and Kelly came over to stand beside her, pushing her glasses up her nose. "This whole thing is insane. You know that, right?"

"I know. But what do you suggest I do?"

"You could say no."

"Yeah, but she would never get over it. At least he's better than Morris Alfred Theobald III."

Kelly snickered and then straightened up as Mitchell and their grandmother entered the room.

He was certainly better-looking than her other suitor. Deanna couldn't deny that.

He looked leisurely and masculine in khakis and a camp shirt. He hadn't bothered to dress up for them, but this didn't surprise Deanna. He definitely seemed like the kind of guy who didn't put himself out more than he had to.

He grinned at her, his smile compelling enough to make her breath hitch just slightly.

She didn't trust men this good-looking. Maybe it meant she was judgmental, but she just couldn't believe it was real.

She smiled back though since she felt her grandmother's wary eyes on her face.

They took their seats as her grandmother made a ceremony about pouring the lemonade for everyone.

Mitchell was looking around at the stuffy, dated room and the multiple collections of memorabilia and clearly didn't have good thoughts about it.

He probably thought the whole lot of them were bizarre anachronisms. Deanna was used to that sort of thing, but it bothered her coming from him.

He was the one who had suddenly announced he was engaged to her. He had no right to judge anyone else's eccentricities.

She straightened her back and tried to keep a passive expression, but she saw Mitchell watching her and suspected she hadn't hidden her annoyance well enough.

It didn't matter. This was his deal. If he wanted to back out of it, he was the one who would be put out the most. Nothing would change about her life except her grandmother would be deeply disappointed.

Mitchell smiled again as he accepted the glass of lemonade. "Thank you. I know this whole situation is a little odd, but I think it might work out to both of our benefits."

He was stating the obvious, probably to open up the topic so this meeting wouldn't last longer than it had to.

That annoyed Deanna too. Her grandmother, as strange as she was, was trying to treat him well, and all he wanted to do was get out of here.

Her grandmother didn't reply until she'd finished handing the glasses of lemonade to Deanna and Kelly.

To fill the silence, Deanna said, "I understand you want to make the restaurant deal with the Fentons, but marriage seems a pretty dramatic step."

Mitchell gave a half shrug. "It's only dramatic if you care about marriage. I don't."

"You don't care about marriage?" Kelly asked, clearly surprised enough to break through her normal reserve with company.

"No. Why would I care? It's just something people do because they've been told to do it. It's a silly remnant from history. Why put that kind of pressure on yourself? People should be together when they want to be together—without all the shackles. To me, it's just a piece of paper, so this arrangement can be purely business. I only commit to temporary relationships anyway. A six-month marriage works just fine for me."

He couldn't have said something more likely to offend the traditional Beauforts if he'd been trying. Maybe he was.

Her grandmother just ignored it though. The lemonade poured, she took her seat and said in a measured voice, "I am sure we can work out some sort of arrangement. As I said last night, we have been trying to restore this house and have found the funding... difficult."

Mitchell nodded, obviously understanding the implication. "I would be happy to help with—" His words broke off as he gave a sudden loud sneeze. "Sorry," he said, blinking and sniffing afterward. "I would be happy to help with the work on your house."

"It is substantial."

Mitchell nodded. "I can see that. I—" He sneezed again, this time wiping his eyes. "I'm sorry. Do you have cat?" He looked around the room warily, as if he suspected one was lurking.

Deanna met Kelly's eyes across the room, both of them thinking of the Pride sitting silently in a row behind the curtain.

But their grandmother just raised her eyebrows and said coolly, "We no longer have pets in this house."

"Okay. Probably just pollen or something." He picked up the napkin that had been set down for his glass and used it to wipe his eyes and nose. "Anyway, I understand there's a lot to be done. I can arrange for a contractor to give an estimate and do the work."

"We would have to agree to it," Deanna said, thinking it might not be beyond him to arrange some sort of under-the-desk deal with a contractor that would leave them with shoddy work.

He gave her a slightly surprised look that was ruined when he sneezed again.

He was definitely allergic to cats. The Pride must be setting him off.

Deanna was about to suggest they move to a different room—even though the other rooms weren't as presentable as this one—when Mitchell said, recovering from the sneeze, "Of course. And I'll have to ensure that only the necessary work is done. Also, I'm not going to mess with all this other clutter."

She sucked in an indignant breath. The asshole was implying they were going to sneak more money out of him than they had to, as if all he owed them for their side of this ridiculous bargain was the bare minimum of their house. And he must be trying to insult them by referring to her grandmother's treasures as "clutter."

She decided not to suggest moving rooms. He could sit in the room with the Pride for a while longer.

He sneezed again, clearly becoming frustrated by the allergy attack. "My lawyers can work out the contract this weekend. Perhaps we can go over the details in a meeting on Monday. The only other thing we need to decide now is how long."

He was definitely impatient to get out of here.

Feeling a malicious spark that wasn't at all typical of her, Deanna looked toward her grandmother. "I don't know. What do you think, Grandmama?"

As she'd expected, the old lady hemmed and hawed for a while. "Good question. There would be various benefits to different time lines. Anywhere from four months to a year might be possible."

Mitchell sneezed three more times as she talked.

"Maybe…" He sneezed again. "What about…" Another sneeze. "Damn it," he muttered, standing up and mopping at his face.

He turned his back toward them and inadvertently faced the closed curtain across the Pride's gallery. "What the hell is wrong…," he muttered after another sneeze.

"What about six months?" Deanna asked, feeling a little stab of pity since he seemed so incredibly uncomfortable suffering from the violence of the allergy attack.

He nodded as he sneezed again. "Good." Then he sneezed two times in a row, bent over double now, tears streaming from his eyes.

No matter how obnoxious he was, she couldn't actually let him get ill from this.

"I'm sorry," she said, standing up and going over to the cord that pulled the curtain. "I just realized what might have triggered the sneezing if you're allergic to cats."

He'd adjusted to face the women, obviously trying to finish the conversation so he could escape, but he turned back around as she pulled the curtain.

Slowly, the row of dead Siamese cats were revealed with their glassy eyes and lifelike expressions.

Mitchell had barely recovered from another sneeze, and he was so taken aback by the unexpected sight that he stumbled backward, away from the uncanny figures.

He stumbled into a side table and knocked four lamps to the floor, the stained glass shade of one of them shattering at the impact with the hardwood floor.

"Oh dear," her grandmother murmured, shaking her head and tsking her tongue. "Oh dear."

Still sneezing, Mitchell gasped, "What… what *are* those things?"

Kelly choked on a burst of hilarity at his reaction and had to run out of the room to keep from laughing in his face.

Deanna was given no such grace. Desperately trying to keep her amusement hidden, she handed Mitchell another napkin. "I'm so sorry," she lied, afraid her eyes might be laughing even as her mouth was perfectly sober. "What a mess. Those are my grandmother's deceased cats. I should have thought of them before and saved you the allergy attack."

Mitchell's eyes were streaming, and he was wiping his face, but she couldn't mistake the cold glare he aimed at her.

He obviously knew she hadn't forgotten about the Pride. He obviously knew she was laughing at him.

And he didn't appreciate it at all.

~

That evening Deanna sat alone on her bed, staring at her phone.

She and Kelly had had a good laugh over poor Mitchell's response to the Pride earlier that afternoon, but the amusement was only temporary. This was a serious situation. She was willing to go to a certain extent to help her family, and she wasn't entirely opposed to a marriage of convenience if it could be treated like a business arrangement, but she had to be very careful.

The upcoming meeting on Monday about the contract with Mitchell's lawyers terrified her.

She knew nothing about contracts. Even if she asked for an explanation of every single clause, she could so easily miss things that would later come back and hurt her or her family.

But there was no way they could afford a lawyer of their own—certainly not one that was good enough to be a match for Mitchell's.

So she'd thought through who she knew and who she could call on for help. They had to keep the real situation of this marriage secret, so she couldn't ask for help from anyone in Savannah. But she'd had a thought.

She was uncomfortable asking for help like this. She'd always resisted doing so. She'd managed to take care of things on her own.

This was too important though, so she swallowed her pride and dialed the number.

When a gruff male voice answered, she said, "Hi, Benjamin. Ben. It's Deanna Beaufort."

"Hey," Benjamin Damon said, a smile in his voice. "How are you?"

"I'm fine. How are you? How's Mandy?"

"We're both good. How about you?"

"I'm okay. I heard you got engaged."

"I did. But I don't think you called me to catch up on the news."

He'd always been like that—even when they'd dated in high school. He could always cut through to the heart of a conversation.

"No. It is good to talk to you, but I actually called for a favor. I hate to ask, but… but I'm kind of desperate."

"Sure. What do you need?"

"I need a lawyer."

There was a pause as he processed this. "Okay. That shouldn't be a problem. What kind of lawyer? Criminal—"

"No, no. Nothing like that. I need someone who can help me negotiate a really important contract."

"What kind of contract?"

"I… I don't think I can tell you that. I'm really sorry. I'm in the strangest sort of situation, and I don't know what to do. But I'm worried that I'll be pressured to sign a contract that isn't good for me, and I need some good legal advice. Do you know someone like that?"

There was now a different sort of smile in Ben's voice. "Absolutely. Actually, I know someone who's great at that. He's in Atlanta this week, if I'm remembering correctly. I can ask if he'll stop by. When is the meeting?"

"Monday. I know it's short notice. I don't want anyone to go out of their way—"

"No, it's totally fine. I'm sure he'll do it. He does contract negotiations better than anyone I've ever met. He'll help you."

Deanna swallowed, touched and overwhelmed and incredibly nervous. "I don't have much money—"

"That won't be a problem. He'll do it as a favor to me."

"Are you sure, Ben? I hate to take advantage of—"

"You're the last person in the world I'd suspect of taking advantage of me. Seriously, Deanna. I spent a lot of years with no one daring to ask me any favors at all. Except Mandy, of course. To tell you the truth, it's nice that you thought I might be willing to help."

~

On Monday morning, Deanna sat in the lobby of the Claremont Inn, waiting for her lawyer to arrive. They'd said she could wait in the conference room, but she wanted to have a few words with her lawyer before she went in to face Mitchell and his, no doubt, powerful team of attorneys.

She was praying this lawyer Ben knew would be nice. And good at his job.

Surely Ben wouldn't have recommended a loser.

She'd told her grandmother that she was going to do this alone since having the old woman there with her would only be a distraction and might bog down negotiations unnecessarily.

Deanna knew what her grandmother wanted. And she knew what she wanted. And she was pretty sure she knew what Mitchell wanted. Hopefully they could work this out without a lot of fuss.

Her lawyer was already seven minutes late. She was holding her breath now, suddenly afraid he couldn't make it.

She'd be woefully unprepared to negotiate a legal document like this on her own.

When she heard the bellboy greet a newcomer, she turned to look, hoping desperately it was the person she was waiting for.

Then she gasped when she saw who it was.

She'd never seen him in person, but she recognized him from pictures and the news. Of course she recognized him.

He just wasn't at all the lawyer she'd expected.

Harrison Damon, Ben's cousin, was well-known in the business world across two continents. He had a JD and an MBA and was the powerhouse negotiator for Damon Enterprises.

He was tall, dark, and as handsome as a movie star in an expensive dark suit. He smiled as he came over to her, obviously knowing who she was.

"Deanna," he said, reaching to shake her hand. "I'm Harrison. Benjamin's cousin."

"I didn't know he was going to send you. I'm sorry to waste your time on something like this."

He shrugged off her apology. "I was in Atlanta anyway. We're opening a new teahouse there. This is only a few hours out of my way. It's no trouble at all."

"Thank you so much."

He looked slightly uncomfortable at her profuse gratitude. "No trouble at all. Benjamin never asks for favors, so I'm really pleased I can do it. Now what kind of cash do you have on you?"

She blinked in surprise, but was too rattled to ask for an explanation. She reached into her purse. "Not much. I always use my debit card—oh, here, I have a ten."

"Give it to me."

She handed him the bill, her eyes wide with confusion.

"Okay." His expression was purely professional, but there was the slightest twitch of amusement at the corner of his fine mouth. "You've now paid for my legal services. I'm your lawyer. Tell me what kind of a mess you've gotten yourself into. It's all protected, so I won't tell anyone."

Ridiculously relieved, Deanna told him the situation as succinctly as she could.

He was impressively cool through her explanation. His eyebrows only lifted slightly.

"I know it's crazy," she concluded.

He studied her closely with lovely chocolate-brown eyes. "You really want to do this?"

She nodded. "I get that you might not understand, but I want to do this… for my grandmother."

He nodded, no amusement at all in his face. "I do understand. I've done crazy things too—out of family loyalty. Just…"

"Just what?"

"You just want to make sure that you're not being pressured to do the wrong thing. That's happened to me before, and not even family loyalty is worth it."

Deanna saw he was serious, and she took a minute to reflect honestly with herself. This was strange. It was awkward. But it didn't feel like the wrong thing. "I don't think it's wrong. Just... weird."

He nodded. "Okay then. Weird, I understand too. No need to justify your choices to me. We'll just make sure the contract is as good for you as it is for him."

She smiled up at him, almost in tears of relief and a surge of hope that they could make this contract work for her and her family.

"Oh, you and your wife had a baby recently, didn't you?" she said, suddenly remembering a detail she'd read in some gossip column.

He almost smiled. "We did. After we finish up here, I'll show you pictures. For now, let's just get this done."

THREE

Mitchell wasn't expecting to see Harrison Damon at the contract meeting, and he wasn't pleased about it.

At all.

He was fine with Deanna bringing an attorney to the proceedings—it made sense, and it wasn't like he wanted her to be taken advantage of—but Damon was different. Damon was a master.

Mitchell had a great business mind, and he had two excellent attorneys with him, but he was going to have to be very careful now that he didn't end up getting the short end of the stick.

This was his idea. He wasn't going to let Damon twist it around to disadvantage him.

He was brewing with attention and adrenalin as Damon and Deanna sat down across the conference table from him. He was so distracted that he barely noticed how pretty and guarded Deanna looked in her slightly old-fashioned skirt and gray top.

He introduced himself to Damon although they'd met briefly a couple of years ago through a mutual business associate.

Damon seemed to remember him, which was a relief. Mitchell's business was peanuts compared to the multibillion-dollar Damon Enterprises, but Mitchell didn't like to think about himself as forgettable.

He gave them both a casual smile that he knew put people off guard. "This should be pretty simple and straightforward. We just need to iron out a few details."

"Of course," Deanna said with a smile of her own, although hers looked rather nervous—as if he was a big bad monster about to devour her.

Mitchell didn't think about himself as a monster, and he didn't appreciate the fact that she clearly believed he was out to get her.

He hid his reaction, however, maintaining the warm smile. He slid a piece of paper over to Deanna. "Here are the terms we'd discussed on Saturday. If we agree to these, then it's just some fine-tuning."

Damon moved the sheet of paper over so he could see it.

"Six months from the wedding date?" he asked after a moment.

"That's what I'd assumed," Mitchell said, relieved the first comment was so unimportant. "But I'm flexible on that if Deanna wants something different."

"That's fine. We're going to get married quickly, right?" she asked. "I don't want to drag this thing out too long."

Mitchell was completely of the same mind and was relieved she didn't want a huge elaborate ceremony that would take months to plan. "We can get married as early as you'd like. Within the next two weeks, if that's good for you. What about the sixteenth?"

He'd already penciled in the wedding for the sixteenth and scheduled out his next six months, but he would rather give in to that than other issues that would cost him more.

"That works for me," Deanna said, looking relieved. Maybe she'd also been afraid he wanted some sort of big hoopla for the wedding. "Just a quick thing at the courthouse or something?"

Mitchell nodded. "Sounds perfect."

Damon had been taking a few notes on the piece of paper as they talked. Mitchell tried not to peer too closely, but it looked like he was doing math equations, which wasn't promising.

Mitchell didn't want to start quibbling about money.

"Since you want the world to believe we're married, I assume you want me to go out in public and act as your wife," Deanna said, not paying attention to whatever notes Damon was taking. "Maybe we can work out what that will look like."

Mitchell smiled, pleased when she smiled back at him. She seemed easygoing enough, and she responded to his attempts to be friendly. He didn't think working with her should be too difficult. "Of course. I don't think it has to be burdensome. Maybe we can agree to go to one public function together a week? I don't keep up a very active society life, so you won't have to be dragged around too often."

"Yes, that's fine."

"And you'll go with her to one public function a week as well, I assume?" Damon asked, not even looking up from his piece of paper.

Mitchell felt a shiver of annoyance toward the other man's evident distraction even though he knew it was just part of a strategy Damon had seen work in business dealings in the past.

He cleared his throat. "I'd be happy to reciprocate, but what kind of public functions do you need to attend?" She didn't seem to be a party animal, and she worked as a receptionist, which wouldn't have a lot of social obligations.

"Well," she said, dropping her eyes as if she were embarrassed, "I know Grandmama would like us to go to church."

Mitchell froze. "You've got to be kidding."

He hadn't been to church since he was eight years old.

Deanna lifted her eyes and met his, suddenly looking not shy at all. The look was almost a challenge.

"It seems reasonable," Damon said calmly. "One public function each a week—whatever it happens to be."

"Fine," Mitchell said, shaking his head at the idea of attending church for the next six months. "I'll just need to know in advance. My schedule is pretty tight, so you can't wake up one morning and spontaneously plan a social outing."

Deanna's silvery green eyes narrowed slightly. "Understood. And the same goes for you, I assume."

"Naturally." He didn't look away from the challenge in her eyes.

There was a long pause as they both stared at each other. Finally, she looked away, and it felt to Mitchell like a victory.

Maybe she was used to manipulating men with her gorgeous eyes and her mild manner, but she would definitely find he wasn't a pushover.

"Okay," Damon said into the silence. "I have a few questions about these numbers."

As Mitchell had feared, Damon's questions turned into concerns, which turned into objections, until the final financial arrangements were much higher than he'd anticipated.

He would pay to restore the old house up to a certain amount, which seemed entirely exorbitant to Mitchell. But then he would also have to match her salary for a year since she would need to give up her job for the six months they were married so she could travel with him when necessary, and then it might take her a while to find another job afterward.

Mitchell couldn't imagine it would take her six months to find another job as a receptionist, but he somehow found himself agreeing to the terms anyway.

He would pay for her lifestyle, of course, but he managed to insist on a monthly allowance rather than just giving her a credit card.

She didn't seem to be a big spender, but then she'd never had money before. Who knew what would happen when she started to shop?

Finally, they'd worked through all the terms Mitchell could think of. The contract was not at all what he'd anticipated it would be, but he could live with it.

It would be worth it if his mother could finally get her restaurant back.

"All right then," he said, leaning back in his chair and feeling almost exhausted from the negotiations. He gave Deanna a cool look. "Is that it then?"

"I think so." She looked over at Damon with trust in her eyes that she'd never shown to Mitchell.

He suddenly wondered if they might be having an affair. He'd always heard Damon was a family man and devoted to his wife, but that could be all talk. Why else would the very busy man fly out of his way to take on such a strange little contract negotiation?

Mitchell didn't like the idea at all. Deanna could sleep with whomever she liked, right up to the time they got married. But then she'd better stop.

As if he'd read his mind, Damon said, "You better talk about sex."

Deanna gave an audible intake of breath, and Mitchell raised his eyebrows.

"Seriously," Damon said, all business, despite the topic of conversation. "You need to work it out beforehand."

"Well, we're not going to have sex, are we?" Deanna asked, her gaze moving from Damon to Mitchell. "I mean, we don't even... know each other."

"But you'll get to know each other. What if you decide you want to later on?"

Deanna looked faintly disgusted, which wasn't at all flattering. "I... I don't think that's going to happen."

"We'll have sex if we both want to, and we won't if one or both of us don't. I don't think that's too hard to work out." Mitchell gave Damon a cold look since the other man was just being difficult now.

"All right. But what about sex outside the marriage?"

"We're not going to have sex outside the marriage, are we?" Deanna said, her eyes very wide now. "I mean, it might just be a business arrangement, but I'm not going to be part of a marriage of any kind where there is cheating."

Mitchell cursed himself for not thinking of something so obvious before. He knew Deanna looked at marriage differently than he did. Where the hell had his mind been? "It wouldn't be cheating if it's agreed upon beforehand," he said gently.

"No." Deanna's shoulders were stiff and her graceful neck high. She obviously took this very seriously, which wasn't surprising given how old-fashioned she was. "If you're planning to have sex with anyone else while we're married, then there won't be a marriage at all. That's a deal breaker for me."

"But you're not willing to have sex with me?"

"I don't foresee it happening, no. So just decide whether getting this restaurant is worth going six months without sex."

Mitchell was angry now—since her terms were entirely unreasonable. He hadn't gone six months without sex since he was a teenager.

But he pulled back his reaction as his mind worked quickly. He wouldn't have to go six months without sex. He was good with women. Deanna seemed to respond to him well enough when they weren't in negotiations. She'd been attracted to him when she'd first seen him at the party. He wasn't blind to that fact.

So he agreed to the terms and let Damon take the lead in fine-tuning the language.

He wouldn't be going six months without sex. He'd get Deanna into his bed soon enough.

~

"You look beautiful," Kelly said, sitting on the bed in Deanna's room and watching as her sister got ready for the engagement party.

"Thanks," Deanna sighed, staring at herself in the mirror. She did look really nice in the new dark red, knee-length dress that showed more cleavage than she was used to. It was the most expensive dress she'd ever owned—bought with Mitchell's money—and it felt strange against her skin.

It didn't feel quite like her. None of this did.

"You might as well enjoy the new clothes and everything," Kelly said, as practical and no-nonsense as ever. "Just think of it as a six-month-long job, and the clothes are all part of the uniform."

"Yeah. That's what I keep telling myself. This is just a business deal. Nothing to worry about."

"That should work, as long as you both look at it that way. Grandmama is in seventh heaven, of course." Kelly paused. "Why do you look worried?"

"I don't know. It's just that sometimes I can't help thinking it's a *marriage*—not a business deal."

"Yeah. There is that."

Deanna forced herself out of her mood, pushing aside the lingering doubts and fears. They'd worked out a very good contract thanks to Harrison's expert help, so she didn't have any worries in that regard.

This was just a job. She was being paid to go through the motions. None of it really compromised who she was. She might as well make the best of it.

"I still wish I could go to the party though," Kelly added.

"I don't want you there," Deanna said baldly, knowing she could speak that way with Kelly without hurting her feelings. "It already seems like a lie, and it would seem more like that if you or Rose were there."

"Fine." Kelly sighed and slumped back against the pillows. "So what is he like?"

"Who?"

"Who do you think? Mitchell."

"Oh." Deanna felt a flush that was entirely unreasonable. There was no reason to feel self-conscious at the thought of him—even though he was going to be her husband.

Yes, he was the most attractive man she'd ever met, and he had a kind of compelling quality that drew people—drew *her*—like a magnet.

But he was also rather self-centered. If she hadn't suspected it before, then she would know it for sure when he wanted to arrange a way for him to have sex with other women while they were married.

She could never be happy with a man who looked at marriage so trivially.

He was a business partner. Nothing else. She would do what she needed to do to get along with him so things would go smoothly, but she wasn't going to let herself like him.

Somehow, she was sure that would be a mistake.

She finally answered her sister. "He's not my kind of guy at all, but I think I can live with him."

~

Their engagement party was a dinner in the private dining room of Mitchell's hotel, the Claremont.

Since their marriage was going to be private, he'd insisted on the engagement party since otherwise people would suspect that something was strange about the marriage.

The guest list was mostly his friends and business associates—most notably the Fentons, who were the people he most needed to convince.

But his sister was there, and Deanna's grandmother and a few of her friends were there as well.

Deanna went through the motions in a kind of daze through the introductions and the meal, keeping a smile on her face that felt faker and faker.

Things would be easier once she got used to it, but right now she felt like some kind of alien who had landed on the wrong planet.

After the meal, people lingered to chat and laugh, and Deanna got cornered by Mitchell's sister, Brie.

Brie looked a lot like her brother—dark hair, gray eyes, classic features, tall build. She had the same warm, charismatic smile, and hers came across as entirely genuine.

"Mitchell told me what's really going on," she said, almost without prelude. She was smiling, but her eyes searched Deanna's face carefully. "It sounds crazy to me."

"It *is* crazy," Deanna agreed, speaking very softly so no one would overhear. "But it seems to work out for both of us."

"You're not being bullied into it, are you?"

"No. Of course, not. Why would you say that?"

"Because it sounded like it was mostly your grandmother's idea and Mitchell's. And I just wanted to make sure you're okay with it all. Mitchell is a great guy—he really is—but when he gets an idea between his teeth, nothing will make him let it go. And he's got this idea to get Mom back the restaurant, and—"

"Wait a minute," Deanna broke in, her curiosity immediately prompted. "The restaurant is for your mom?"

"Of course." Brie looked surprised. "Didn't you know that? Why do you think he's going to such great lengths here? My mom started as a cook at the Darlington Café—almost forty years ago now. She was the one who made it such a success. She poured her heart and soul into it. But then the owner sold it to the Fentons, and she lost her job. Mitchell is on this mission to get it back for her."

Deanna experienced a swell of feeling, her eyes resting on Mitchell across the room. He was talking to one of his friends, looking as casual and insouciant as ever.

But he loved his mother. He loved her so much that he was doing this ridiculous thing to make her happy.

He might be cool and distanced and kind of arrogant, but Lucy Damon had been right. He loved his mother.

That went a long way for Deanna.

"Didn't you know that?" Brie asked again, evidently seeing something in Deanna's expression. "Why did you think he was doing this?"

"I don't know. I thought it was just a business deal. I thought…" She trailed off. "I'm glad to know," she said with a smile. "His mother isn't here tonight?"

Brie smiled back, and Deanna felt like they'd made a real connection. They were around the same age. Maybe they

49

could even be friends. "No. She lives in Florida with my aunt. He's not telling her about the marriage yet because she'd figure out why he was doing it and get upset. He wants to surprise her with the restaurant after it's over."

"Does it really mean that much to her?"

"I don't know. It means a lot, but I think it means more to Mitchell. Some sort of gesture of devotion. He's just got it between his teeth and won't let it go."

"I think it's kind of cool," Deanna admitted.

"So you're really okay with this?" Brie asked again.

"Yes, I'm really okay. It's just six months. It's not like it's a forever thing. We can be professional about it."

"Yeah. I guess that's true."

Deanna's eyes were still on Mitchell as she tried to process this new knowledge of him.

He seemed more real than he had before—like there was a heart and soul inside the fine body—and her attraction for him intensified even more.

He noticed her watching him and smiled. It was probably just for show, but the smile was intimate, and prompted a little shudder of pleasure inside her.

It was so strange—so crazy—to think he would be her husband.

And it was nice to know he wasn't too bad of a guy.

He walked over to her, and he slid an arm around her as he approached, pulling her against his side.

Obviously, it was done to convince the onlookers that they were really in love, but it felt nice.

He was big and warm and strong and masculine, and it was hard not to enjoy the feel of him against her.

Everyone was smiling as they looked on.

"Oh, how the mighty have fallen," someone said—a middle-aged man who was some sort of business associate of Mitchell's. "After all your talk of not believing in marriage, you surrender the moment you fall in love."

Deanna felt Mitchell stiffen slightly, which was interesting, but the smile never left his face. "I admit it. I was a goner from the very beginning." He leaned down and pressed his lips against Deanna's, and she felt a shiver of response.

The kiss was fake. Of course it was. She couldn't help but respond to it anyway.

There was some more laughter and some more teasing, and Deanna drank one too many glasses of champagne. She felt a little fuzzy and overly warm when people started to leave.

"Well, that seemed to go well," Mitchell murmured. He was still standing beside her, his arm around her once again. There were only a few people left in a conversation across the room.

"Yeah. They all seem completely taken in. Either we're good actors, or people are pretty gullible."

"Probably both." He was speaking low, so his mouth was close to her ear, and she felt another spiral of pleasure and attraction rise up inside her.

If she had to marry a man for a weird fake reason, Mitchell wasn't a bad one to end up with.

"How are you feeling about everything?" he asked.

It was nice of him to ask, and his gray eyes were serious and attentive, like he really cared. She'd been wrong about him at first. He wasn't really as thoughtless and selfish as she'd thought.

She couldn't get over the fact that he was doing all this for his mother.

"I'm fine. I think it's all going to be fine. I think we'll be able to get along just fine."

She was saying "fine" a lot. Too much. She couldn't look away from his deep eyes, and his face was getting closer and closer to her.

And she wanted it to. The scent of him—masculine and real somehow—filled her senses, and her heart was beating like crazy in her chest.

She wanted him to kiss her. Again. And not just for show.

"I think so too," he murmured, his voice definitely husky.

His face drifted closer to hers until his lips brushed against her mouth, very gently. "I think we'll get along very well," he murmured, just before he kissed her again.

It wasn't a deep kiss, but it lingered. Deanna's mind roared with excitement and pleasure as her hands rose unconsciously to cling to the lapels of his jacket. Her breath hitched when he took her bottom lip, very gently, between his teeth and gave it a little tug.

The sharp desire that tightened inside her was impossible to mistake. She was trembling as she tried to press herself against him.

A laugh across the room distracted them, and Mitchell pulled away.

The remaining guests had caught them kissing and thought it was funny. Deanna found it frustrating.

The laughter reminded her it was fake, which was weird enough. But mostly she wasn't pleased with the interruption.

Maybe sex shouldn't be as off the table as she'd originally assumed.

~

An hour later, Mitchell was waiting for Deanna to come out of the bathroom so he could drive her home.

She said she could just go home with her grandmother, but Mitchell thought it would look better and more natural if he took her home himself.

Mitchell was surprisingly tired after the evening, but everything had gone smoothly.

Everyone was convinced. Gina Fenton was convinced. And Deanna was definitely proving to be amenable to his advances.

His phone rang as he waited, and he picked it up when he saw it was Brie.

"Hey," he said. "What's up?" He certainly wasn't expecting a call when she'd just left the party.

"Just calling to tell you once more that I think this is a very bad idea."

"I know that's what you think." Mitchell sighed and walked out onto a terrace so Deanna wouldn't overhear if she happened to come out of the bathroom before he expected her to. "But I think it's going to work out fine."

"Someone is going to get hurt, and I think it's going to be Deanna."

"You talked to her, didn't you? I assume she didn't tell you she was forced into this against her will."

"No, of course not. But that doesn't mean she won't get hurt."

"I'm not going to hurt her. What the hell do you think I'm going to do to her?"

"You're going to be your normal charming self, and she's going to fall for you, thinking it's real."

"She knows it's not real. I've been nothing but honest with her."

Against his will, Mitchell remembered how she'd felt against him when he kissed her. She was absolutely delectable, and she'd been warm and passionate—responding to the slightest of his touches.

He was already dying to get her into bed. He didn't think it would take very long.

"Yeah, but knowing is different than *knowing*. I saw you two tonight. Please don't hurt her. She seems really nice."

"I'm not going to hurt her. Give me a little credit, damn it. We've both been honest about everything."

"Yeah, but that doesn't mean it won't get complicated."

Mitchell stared out at the lush gardens that his staff carefully tended. The lighter blooms of flowers glowed in the moonlight. "It's not going to get complicated."

"That's what you say now, but people are complicated, and I don't think she's as much of a pushover as you think."

"I don't think Deanna is a pushover. But I don't think she'll be difficult. She's smart enough, but she's... she doesn't have a lot of backbone."

He thought about her at the negotiations—her stiff shoulders and gracefully held neck—but she was only that way because she had Harrison Damon at her side.

She wouldn't have a champion in their marriage. She wasn't going to cause him any trouble.

"That's not very nice, Mitchell."

"I know, but it's true. She does what she's told. She'll be easy to manage."

A slight sound behind him had him whirling around, and he felt a cold, stark chill when he saw Deanna at the door to the terrace.

But he relaxed when he saw she was just opening it. She was smiling at him and looked perfectly composed.

She hadn't overheard.

That was good. Mitchell might not be particularly sensitive, but he didn't actually want to hurt her feelings.

He wasn't the nicest guy in the world, but he didn't like to think of himself as heartless.

FOUR

Deanna and Mitchell got married at four o'clock in the afternoon on the following Saturday. He wore a charcoal gray suit, and she wore a pretty, simple cream-colored dress that fell to midcalf since she would have felt stupid in a real wedding gown for a mostly fake wedding at the courthouse.

She carried a small bouquet of pink tulips and spent most of the short ceremony telling herself not to claw the obnoxious smile off his handsome face.

She hadn't seen him much for the past week since they were both busy—him with work and her with preparations for moving into his house and finishing up at her job. She'd been brooding on the conversation she'd overheard at the party all week though.

He thought she was weak. Spineless. *Easy to manage.*

And what made it worse was his charming act at the party had started to work on her, proving that he was partly right.

He wasn't completely right though. She did hate to say no to the people she cared about, and she'd done a lot out of loyalty to her grandmother. But she wasn't as malleable as he seemed to think she was, and he'd find out how wrong he was soon enough.

It didn't help that she found him just as attractive today as she had last week. Even the knowledge of what he really thought of her didn't change how appealing, how compelling she found his handsome face, his strong, masculine body, the charisma that always lurked under the surface of his persona even when he wasn't letting it out.

She wasn't going to be fooled by the attraction again though.

She kept a smile on her face as they repeated simple vows and Mitchell slid a sleek, modern wedding band on her hand. It felt weird as he did so. His eyes never left her face, and he held her small hand like it was crystal—but obviously it didn't mean anything.

He was good with women. He obviously always had been. He assumed he could be good with her too and get her to do anything he wanted. Deanna had always been proud—taught to be so by her grandmother and forced to be so by a family that others found to be a source of amusement. She was certainly too proud to let Mitchell Graves be proven right about her.

She pulled her hand away from his as soon as she could since the feel of his warm fingers against her skin was disturbing.

She felt his eyes on her face, but she held on to her smile. Then they paused for a few pictures as evidence of their matrimonial reality.

They hadn't invited anyone else to the wedding. The story would be they decided not to wait and just got married quietly without a big fuss. Deanna was glad. Marrying Mitchell would feel more like a lie if her family and friends had been present.

"Is everything all right?" he asked quietly, leaning down to murmur into her ear as they walked out into the lobby.

She carefully pulled back from him so his lips weren't quite so close to her face. "Yes, of course." She smiled at him, desperately trying to look relaxed and casual, even though a chill of anxiety was shivering up and down her spine. "Why wouldn't it be?"

"I don't know. You just seem... stiff or upset or something." He was still studying her face, looking for evidence of what he sensed in her mood.

She understood what he was picking up from her— she must have been sending out vibes that she didn't like him, she didn't want to be close to him. It was true, but there was no sense in bursting out with it since they were stuck in this marriage now.

She was his bride—bought and paid for so the Beauforts could rebuild their ancestral home.

She had to do a better job of fooling him. They'd be seeing each other a lot now. This afternoon she'd be moving into his house. She'd have her own suite of rooms. That was already arranged. But they'd be living together and going about as man and wife—obviously, they'd run into each other a lot.

She willed herself to act natural as she smiled again. "I'm not upset. Honestly, I'm a little... a little nervous about this whole thing. It's strange, you know."

His smile widened again, nearly taking her breath away since it appeared genuine. "I know. It's very strange. But I think it will be fine. Nothing to be nervous about. Do you want to go get something to eat or just head home?"

Home. His home, not hers, although she'd be living there for the next six months. She wouldn't even have much of her own stuff there. She'd already moved over the few possessions she was taking with her. All her clothes would be new—to suit the wardrobe of a wife of Mitchell Graves.

She wished now she'd brought all her beads. At least that would have given her something to do—something that brought her joy. She'd left them because they hadn't seemed to fit with her life as Mitchell's wife, but now she realized that was ridiculous. She was still herself, even married to him.

She suddenly decided there was no reason not to get them. "Do you mind if we stop back at my house first?" she asked. "I need to pick something up. I can go myself, if you'd rather." She didn't own a car. She'd never been able to afford one. She could take a taxi if she needed one, but she figured he might still be playing his charming role and would insist on taking her himself.

He wanted her compliant. It was too early for him to start distancing himself. He didn't have her wrapped around his finger completely yet.

His eyes widened. "Sure. Of course. I thought you already brought things over though."

"I did. I was going to leave some stuff behind, but I just changed my mind. It's fine if you'd—"

"I can take you," he interrupted, frowning as if he didn't appreciate the assumption he wasn't considerate enough to take her. "It's not that far out of the way. As long as I don't have to go into the room with those dead cats."

The Beauforts lived in one of the historic neighborhoods at the heart of the city. Most of the houses were gorgeously restored, and all of them were old and stately, on streets lined with oaks and Spanish moss.

Mitchell lived in a gated community in the south of the city with new houses, large pieces of property, and plenty of privacy.

The Beaufort home wasn't anywhere close to Mitchell's, and it was definitely out of the way, but Deanna didn't bother argue. He was trying to be nice so she'd fall for him even more.

When they arrived, Deanna saw a flutter of curtains in the parlor, so she knew her someone had seen them drive up.

Kelly opened the door before Deanna could turn the knob. "Are you married?" she demanded.

Deanna shook her head and raised her hand so her sister could see the simple platinum band next to the engagement ring with the diamond solitaire Mitchell had presented her with last week. She would have preferred a ring with more history and character than the sleek modern lines, but Mitchell had bought the rings, and he'd obviously chosen what he liked. "The deed is done."

"How strange does it feel?" Kelly asked.

Deanna chuckled. "Pretty strange." She glanced up at Mitchell, catching him watching her closely again.

She wondered what was going on in his mind. Did he recognize that she wasn't as compliant as she'd been last week? Was he starting to plot to make sure he got her back under his thumb, easy to manage once more?

A sudden brainstorm hit her—the kind of spark of naughty genius that almost never tempted her. But she couldn't resist, remembering how condescendingly he'd spoken of her on the phone call.

She gave him a warmer smile. "But I think it's going to be okay."

His face visibly relaxed. "I think so too."

"Grandmama isn't here," Kelly informed them, giving them both curious looks. "She's having tea with Mrs. Endicott. She'll be very upset about missing you."

Mitchell's face relaxed even more, and Deanna knew he wasn't at all upset about missing her grandmother.

"We're not here to visit," Deanna told her sister. "I just decided I wanted my beads after all."

"Oh, okay." Kelly followed them as they walked up the staircase. "That's probably a good idea. You'll be kind of bored, won't you, sitting around in a fancy house with nothing to do."

"My house isn't that fancy," Mitchell said, glancing over his shoulder in a friendly way. "And she's welcome to do anything she likes with her time."

Deanna could think of a few things she might do that he would have objections to, but she didn't mention them. "That's really nice of you," she murmured instead, lowering her eyelids in what she hoped was a shy look.

Mitchell was definitely looking less concerned now, and Kelly was looking very confused.

Fortunately, her sister didn't say anything.

When they reached Kelly's bedroom, Mitchell paused in the doorway at the sight of all the tins of beads and spools of wire that were scattered over the floor. "Wow," he breathed. "What are all these for?"

"I like to make jewelry and little purses and stuff with beads." She opened her closet and found a little beaded coin purse she'd made two years ago. "Like this, see?"

He took the purse in both his hands, staring down at it. Deanna had been proud of that one since it had taken forever to get the roses to look right on it, and she couldn't help but be pleased when his expression showed that he was impressed. "You made this?"

"Yeah." She tried to look bashful and simpering, as he would expect her to. "It's just a little hobby I have."

It wasn't a little hobby. She loved working with beads, and she sometimes dreamed of making a living at it.

"This is really good. You make jewelry too? Have you tried to do anything with your stuff?"

"Yeah. I sell it online, and a few local shops will stock some of my better items. So far, it's only brought in pocket money though."

"Well, it's a start." He was looking down at the beaded coin purse, and his expression now was thoughtful. "We can put a shelf of some of your stuff in the Claremont shop if you want. This is good enough to place there, and people at hotels buy all kinds of useless stuff they wouldn't otherwise." His head jerked up. "Not that it's useless. I didn't mean that. I just mean it's pretty stuff, not practical stuff."

Deanna laughed. She couldn't help it. He looked so guilty and worried by his gaff, although she actually liked him better for it since he didn't seem so fake and practiced. "I know what you meant. And, thank you. I would love to put some stuff in the shop if you think it would be of interest. I'll have to make some more first though since I've sold most of my best stuff already."

"Sure. Anytime."

They smiled at each other, both of them clearly pleased by this arrangement, and Deanna suddenly remembered that she couldn't fall under his thrall again.

She would need to be careful. It felt like the spontaneous offer was genuine and wasn't part of his charming act, but he would use it for sure, and she couldn't let him succeed in wooing her.

As if he'd read her mind, he slipped an arm around her waist and smiled down at her in that intimate way, the expression that was supposed to leave her weak and boneless. Even now, knowing what he was doing, it almost worked. "I had no idea my new bride was so talented," he said.

She had to fight the instinct to pull away. Instead, she gave a silly giggle. "I'm not that talented. Thank you though."

When she glanced up, she saw that Kelly was looking at her suspiciously. Her sister would know this was not normal behavior for her, and she would wonder why. "Well, let's start gathering all this stuff up," Kelly said, fortunately not asking about Deanna's actions. "Just be careful. We don't want another bead spill. Remember last time?"

Deanna shuddered at the memory of her grandmother knocking over a tin of beads in the back sitting room, where Deanna had been working on them. It had been months before they'd found them all.

She could just picture Mitchell's face if tiny little beads ended up rolling all over his no doubt immaculate, modern house. He would hate that.

In fact, if he got too obnoxious, she could always arrange for a little accidental bead spill. It would be a good thing to keep in her pocket.

For now though, he wasn't being too smarmy, although he smiled at her too much and gave her a few more compliments when she showed him her jewelry. The three of them managed to pack a few boxes with all her supplies, and then the girls let Mitchell carry them down to the car since he insisted.

"What's going on?" Kelly whispered when he carried the first two boxes down at one time.

"What do you mean?" Deanna knew what her sister was talking about, but she acted innocent.

"You know. I assume you haven't miraculously fallen in love in a couple of hours. Why are you acting that way?"

"What way?"

"I don't know. All silly and giggly."

Deanna raised her eyebrows. "I have my reasons."

Kelly snickered. "Do you have some sort of wicked plot going on?"

"Maybe."

"He really got on your bad side," Kelly said. "I haven't seen you look like this since Melissa Larsen told your whole class that you'd slept with her boyfriend. What did Mitchell do?"

"Nothing. It's not like that." Although it was exactly like that.

"Seriously, what did he—"

"Nothing," Deanna said quickly, waving a hand when she heard Mitchell coming into the house again. "Now, shh. Don't say anything."

Deanna was smiling sweetly as Mitchell came up again, and this time Kelly was smiling sweetly too.

He pulled to a stop, looking at them warily. "What's going on?" he asked, looking from one to the other.

"Nothing," Deanna assured him, wishing her sister wasn't smiling quite so fakely.

"Were you talking about me?"

"Maybe a little." She took his arm to pull him back into the bedroom so he couldn't start to interrogate Kelly. "It's not every day that a girl has a marriage of convenience, and it's natural her sister might want to hear about it."

Mitchell chuckled as he picked up the last box. His hair was slightly mussed, and he was sweating slightly in the heat. He looked even more attractive than he had before. "Maybe I *want* to hear about it."

"Well, you can't." She gave him a little swat, hoping that was something an easy-to-manage wife might do, and she followed him down the stairs, wanting to get out before her grandmother returned.

If Grandmama arrived, they'd have to do the niceties, which would mean they'd be stuck here for another hour at least.

Mitchell didn't linger, so maybe he had the same idea, and soon they were on their way south toward his house, the boxes of beads in the back of his car.

They were stopped at a light when she recognized that Mitchell's gaze was on her face again.

"What?" she asked, pushing her hair behind her ear and not having to pretend the feeling of self-consciousness.

"You look beautiful today," he said, his voice huskier than normal.

She dropped her eyes. She'd expected this. It was clearly part of the nice act he was putting on to keep her doing his bidding. "Thank you."

"I've never seen anyone with eyes like yours before."

She'd actually heard this from other people—her eyes were a very unusual shade of light green—so it was possible that he meant it. "I always hated them when I was a kid. I had teachers who used to think I was wearing eye makeup since my eyes were so light and my eyelashes so dark."

"They're gorgeous. All of you is gorgeous."

She blushed, and it was for real since there was a note in his voice she couldn't help but like. Almost a caress.

She reminded herself to get a grip though.

She couldn't forget that he hadn't been pleased by the prospect of six months without sex. He would want to have sex, and he wouldn't be able to go outside their marriage to get it.

Which meant he would want to have sex with her. He'd agreed too quickly at the contract negotiations. He probably thought she would easily succumb to his advances, and her behavior at the engagement party must have confirmed this fact.

He no doubt believed that he'd have no trouble talking her into sex with him tonight. She wasn't opposed to letting him believe so for now. Let him think she was every bit as silly and spineless as he assumed.

It was Mitchell who would be surprised and disappointed when he spent his wedding night alone.

~

After a brief flicker of concern when Deanna acted so skittish at the wedding, Mitchell was pleased with how things were going.

Deanna was easy to get along with, and she seemed to get more beautiful every time he saw her. It wouldn't be hard to work out an arrangement that worked for him—a wife who didn't cause him any trouble and a willing sex partner.

He was getting more excited about the sex partner idea as the evening went on.

They'd gotten to his place, and he'd carried her beads into the sitting room of her suite, which he'd had fixed up for her last week. Deanna seemed happy with everything, and they'd both been in good moods after they'd showered, rested, and had dinner together on the terrace that overlooked the river.

Mitchell asked her about her beadwork since he was sincerely interested in it and impressed by how good she was at it. Then she asked about his family, and he told her some about his sister and mother.

She seemed to want to hear about his mother's history with the Darlington Café. He'd started by only sharing a few minor details, but at her questions he told her more until he was spilling all kinds of stuff he wasn't in the habit of talking about—including how his mother would come back from working at the restaurant late when he was just a boy and he'd be awake so she'd fix them both pancakes.

They split a bottle of wine, so he was relaxed and satisfied as they fell into silence. The breeze brought with it the tang of salt and the sweetness of magnolias from the tree at the corner of the house. Deanna's eyes looked huge and otherworldly as they gazed up at him, and he couldn't help but wonder what she was thinking.

Despite her docile demeanor, she seemed to have depth, like there was far more going on under the surface than she ever revealed to the world.

He wanted to know what it was, what was simmering under the surface. He wanted it to break the delicate prettiness of her quietude.

He put down his glass and shook himself off slightly, looking away from her at last. What the hell was he even thinking? He'd like to get her into bed. That was probably all that was prompting his weird, intense thoughts.

It was still early—not even eight. Usually he worked out in the evenings, but if Deanna would like to go straight to bed, he would have no objections.

"What do you do in the evenings?" he asked.

She gave a little shrug. "It depends. There were always jobs to do around the house. It was really falling down around our heads. But otherwise, I'd just do some beads and watch TV or something."

"Well, you're welcome to do that here if you'd like. You can watch the big screen one downstairs if you want."

If she went into her own suite and closed the door, it would be harder to ease into sex.

"Okay. Thank you!" She beamed at him, and he felt another surge of desire overtake him along with that feeling from before of wanting to know what was really going on under the surface.

It had been a long time since he'd been as consumed by lust as this. He wasn't even sure where it was coming from.

An hour later, they were both in the media room, seated on the floor in front of the couch.

Mitchell wasn't actually a fan of sitting on the floor, but Deanna had set up her beads there, and he wanted to sit next to her.

She hadn't brought all the tins of beads down—just one that seemed to be a random mix of all different colors and styles. She was working on what she told him would be a fancy clutch, but she'd just started so he had no way of ascertaining what the finished product would look like.

He watched her though as much as she watched the old movie she'd turned on.

Her hands were tiny, but they worked incredibly fast, threading the beads in an arrangement she must be able to see in her mind. She would bite her bottom lip as she concentrated, and he was mesmerized by the little gesture. He was also mesmerized by the way her camisole kept dipping to expose a hint of cleavage.

She'd changed into her pajamas before she'd come to watch television, which was perfectly amenable to Mitchell.

He'd asked her questions to begin with, but now he was just watching. She'd look up occasionally, and her eyelashes would flutter down when she realized he was focused on her.

After more than an hour, she caught him looking again and burst out, "Why do you keep staring at me?"

It was a perfectly good opening. He wasn't going to let it slide by. "Because you're too gorgeous not to look at."

"That's ridiculous. I'm not that gorgeous."

"I beg to differ." He reached over and cupped one of her cheeks, his hand looking big and rough against her delicate skin. "I've never seen anyone as gorgeous as you. I don't know how it happened. It just seemed to sneak up on me. I thought you were pretty the first time we met, but now I can't keep my eyes off you."

He hadn't intended to say quite so much—all of it absolutely true—but it seemed to work at least. She blushed deeply, dropping her eyes once more, only to lift them again in that alluring way. His breath actually hitched with a tightening of desire just from the provocation of her expression.

"I think you're full of it," she said, her voice wobbling slightly, proof that she was responding to him.

"I'm full of something," he admitted, "But it's not what you think."

She blinked, and her mouth parted to say something, but he couldn't hold back anymore. Still cupping her cheek, he leaned down to kiss her fully on the mouth.

She made a little whimpering sound, frozen for a few moments as his lips moved against hers. Then something seemed to crack or uncoil inside her. She let out a little moan and grabbed at his neck, holding on as he deepened the kiss.

His blood was coursing with excitement as he gathered her small, lush body in his arms, pulling her up so she was straddling his lap, which was the only comfortable way of kissing her on the floor like this. Then she was all over him, sucking his tongue into her mouth, wrapping her arms around his neck, rubbing herself against him.

She felt warm and real and eager and passionate in his arms, and it drove him into deeper need. He wanted to devour her, swallow her whole. His groin was aching with a pulsing need that drove him well beyond thought.

She wanted him too. He could feel it. He wasn't sure he could go much longer without having her.

The kiss finally broke, and she whimpered again as she dropped her head back, exposing the lovely line of her neck for his enjoyment. He leaned forward to nibble a trail down it, pausing to mouth at her pulse.

She squirmed, obviously as turned on as he was. He moved his arms so he could hold on to her, spanning the curve of her ribs with his hands just under her breasts. She arched into him, flushed and responsive and causing his already-hard erection to throb dangerously in his pants.

He wasn't going to be able to wait much longer. He needed to have her. Now.

"Can I take you to bed?" he asked, surprised by how breathless he sounded.

She gave a little moan, rubbing herself against the bulge in his pants, obviously wanting the friction. But then something changed in her body—tightened, cooled down—and she was climbing off his lap. "No. I don't think so."

"Wait," he said, reaching out for her again, "What are you doing?"

"Sorry about all this," she said, hiding her eyes—in a different way than she'd been doing before. "I didn't mean to let it go so far. I was—I don't know what happened, but I'm sorry."

"Why are you sorry? Why do we have to stop?" He was starting to come to a bleak realization that things weren't going exactly as he'd envisioned them this evening.

"I don't want to have sex." She put the work she'd done in the tin with the beads, her fingers trembling visibly.

He almost choked. "Yes, you do. You were as into things as I was. What the hell is going on?"

"I'm sorry," she said again, not meeting his eyes as she straightened up. "I didn't mean to be that kind of tease. I just… I don't want to have sex. I'm going to bed."

"*What?* Deanna, what—" He broke off as she jumped to her feet. He stood up too, reaching out for her again. "Tell me why we can't have sex when we obviously both want to."

"I don't want to. Not really. Just let me go." She jerked her arm out of his grip, and the move surprised him. He stepped backward, knocking into the tin of beads, which hadn't been fully closed.

The tin jerked violently, and about half the beads spilled out, rolling out in all directions in a huge mess on the smooth hardwood floor.

Mitchell groaned. "Deanna!" His arousal was throbbing almost painfully now, and it was obviously not going to be satisfied in the way he wanted.

She was almost at the door, but she turned to say over her shoulder. "I said I'm sorry. I really didn't mean to go that far. But maybe…" She made a strange choking sound. "Maybe I'm not a wife who is as easy to manage as you thought."

FIVE

The next morning, Deanna felt like crap.

She felt horrible about the night before. She'd always intended to lead him on to a certain extent—make him think he was succeeding before pulling the rug out from under him—but she'd never planned to let it go so far.

Once he'd started to kiss her, it was like something came alive inside her, something that couldn't be stopped.

She'd come to her senses eventually. Just in time. She'd been on the brink of surrendering everything to him, which would have been a mistake she might never have recovered from. But then she felt like a heartless tease, leaving him turned on that way.

She let her breath out as she stared at the ceiling of an unfamiliar bedroom. Oh well. Nothing to do about it. It was done. She'd apologize this morning and try to do better in the future.

No matter how mad he made her or how condescending he acted toward her, no more games. This was real life. They both were real people who could be hurt. And there could be consequences she didn't foresee.

With this resolved in her mind, she felt better about the whole situation, and she got up to take a shower. There was a coffee maker in her sitting room, so she made herself a cup to drink as she got dressed. It was Sunday, so she pulled on capris and a knit top, wondering what on earth she was supposed to do with herself today in this big unfamiliar house.

If she got too bored, she could always go visit her family. She reminded herself of this as she pulled her hair back in a low ponytail and ventured out of her pretty suite.

She wandered around until she practically ran into Mitchell. He must have been working out because he was soaked with sweat, so much that his shirt was sticking to his chest and moisture dripped down the sides of his face.

He still managed to look sexy, but she made herself ignore this fact.

"Morning," she said with an apologetic smile.

"Hi." He was studying her closely, the way he had at the wedding the day before, as if he were still trying to figure her out.

Wanting to get the whole thing over with, she burst out, "Sorry about last night."

At exactly the same time, he burst out, "Sorry about everything."

They stared at each other in surprise.

"What are you sorry about?" she asked at last, feeling rattled and even more attracted to him now that he looked almost sheepish—much more sincere than anything she'd seen from him before.

He let out a breath. "Obviously, you overheard what I was saying to Brie last week at the party."

She stared at the floor. "Oh. Yeah. I did."

"I'm sorry I said it. It was an asshole thing to say."

"You didn't know I would overhear."

"Yeah, but still… I was wrong, but even if I wasn't, I feel bad about it. You shouldn't have had to hear that from me."

She glanced up at him to check his expression, and he didn't appear to be trying to play her with his charm the way he'd been doing the day before. He seemed real. Like this was really him. Like he meant what he said.

She had to start believing him, or they'd never make it through the next six months. She nodded. "Thank you. For the apology, I mean. And I'm really sorry about last night."

"You said that last night."

"I know, but I want to say it again, now that we're not both... so distracted. I never meant for that to happen. I never would have... teased you like that."

"I'm glad." He sounded serious and looked it when she focused up at him again. "I still don't know why you're so against having sex."

"I'm not totally against it," she began. At his raised eyebrows, she added, "Okay. I was since I thought you were... you weren't being nice." She almost caught a twitch of his lips that was remarkably appealing. "But I still don't think it's a good idea. We don't really know each other, and this is going to be hard enough without the complications of sex. I think we need to just focus on making this situation work... at least for the time being."

She hadn't meant to add the last bit, but she was starting not to like the idea of closing the door to sex with him completely.

She kind of wanted to touch him now. She remembered well how it had felt to touch and be touched by him last night. She'd never felt anything like it before in her life.

"Okay," he said lightly. "I don't think it would have to make things complicated—I think we could both just enjoy it for what it is—but we can hold off for now. But we definitely want to avoid a repeat of last night."

"Of course." She gave a firm nod. "So maybe we should agree to not even kiss unless other people are around and we're playing the part."

"You're big on making rules, aren't you?" He appeared to be hiding a smile now, so she knew he wasn't annoyed.

She frowned since she had never thought of herself that way. "Not really. I just think it's smart to get things straight between us. Last night wasn't... wasn't any fun."

"No. It definitely wasn't." He paused, studying her face again. "So we're all right? About everything, I mean?"

She nodded again. "Yes, I think we're all right. We've got to make this work, so we might as well be reasonable and adult about it and try to get along."

"Sounds like a plan to me. And speaking of, do you want to go to Charleston next week? I've got to go anyway, so it might be fun for you to come along. We can call it a honeymoon."

She narrowed her eyes at the word, until he said with a low chuckle. "Not that kind of honeymoon. Just a trip you might enjoy. You don't have to come if you don't want to."

"No, I'll come," she said, excited about the idea and excited that he seemed to be so funny and nice when he was being himself. "I've always wanted to go to Charleston, but we never had the money. There's all kind of history there."

"Great." He grinned at her. "We'll leave on Friday if that's okay with you."

"That sounds great."

"Okay." He wiped his forehead with the back of his forearm. "I better go to take a shower before I drip all over the floor."

She watched him go, enjoying the view of his long legs and tight butt, but only after he disappeared did she remember that he'd never agreed to the no-kissing-in-private rule.

~

On Wednesday, for the weekly public function he was required to attend with Deanna, Mitchell had to go to afternoon tea at her grandmother's.

On the first invitation, he thought he had a good excuse for bowing out since he was deathly allergic to those morbid dead cats of hers. The memory of the sneezing attack and then the revelation of the stuffed corpses of so many Siamese cats all in a row still gave him shivers.

But his excuse was a no-go since Deanna said sweetly that her grandmother was hosting it in the garden and his allergies wouldn't be a problem.

So Mitchell bit back his reluctance and his dozens of reasons not to go—including the fact that it was in the middle of a workday—and said that would be fine.

It was written into the contract, after all. Deanna had attended a cocktail party with him this week, so he had to go to afternoon tea with her.

Evidently, he also had to dress for the occasion.

That was why he ended up sitting in an uncomfortable wrought iron chair in the garden of the dilapidated Beaufort house, wearing a tan suit that was way too hot for the heat and humidity of the afternoon, waving away the flies and trying to make polite conversation with Mrs. Beaufort and her cohorts—three other equally elderly Southern ladies.

At least he was being served iced tea instead of hot tea.

Deanna, pretty in a pale green casual cotton dress, was sitting demurely and replying pleasantly to all the comments aimed at her—and sometimes him. But occasionally he saw her slanting a discreet gaze over to him, as if she were checking him out.

He wasn't sure whether she was critiquing his performance or enjoying his discomfort until he saw her lips purse in suppressed amusement.

She was definitely enjoying it.

"Where is your family from, young man?" one of the other ladies asked him.

He gave a slight shrug. "Here and there, I think. My mother was born in Savannah, and my father was just passing through." He'd never known his father. He'd never wanted to know him since the man was obviously an ass who'd not cared that he'd gotten a woman of no means pregnant.

When he heard a couple of the women gasp, he looked over at Deanna, but she didn't look annoyed or embarrassed by his comment. She was looking at him interestingly. "Did you ever know anything about him?"

He shook his head. "He was a salesman. From up north somewhere. That's all I know."

"Did your mother ever marry?" she asked.

"Deanna," her grandmother hissed. "Don't be gauche."

Deanna looked surprised. "But he's my husband. It's not gauche to ask your husband personal questions, is it?"

"You should know more about him already, dear," one of the women said with a maternal smile. "Don't you two ever talk over your histories?"

Mitchell met Deanna's eyes. "We've been talking about other things," he said with a slight lilt to his tone.

The women—except Deanna and her grandmother—tittered, evidently thinking his comment was somehow daring, and Deanna hid another smile.

"Shall I bring some more tea out, Grandmama?" she asked, standing up and reaching for the mostly empty glass pitcher.

"Yes, dear. Thank you."

"Do you want to help, Mitchell?" she asked, glancing at him over her shoulder.

He wasn't sure why refilling the pitcher would take two people, but he jumped at the opportunity to escape for a few minutes.

He took the pitcher from her hands as they walked back into the house by the back door that led into the kitchen.

"How are you holding up?" she asked, giving him an amused smile.

He didn't like being the source of such amusement for her, but he did like the sight of that particular smile. "I'm fine. Did you think I would fall apart in the face of such a polite interrogation?"

"No. I thought you might get fed up and storm out."

"I'm not that rude." He took a less attractive pitcher of ice tea from the refrigerator and started to pour the liquid into the fancy pitcher.

She arched her eyebrows as she held the crystal pitcher but didn't say anything.

"I'm not rude," he said, feeling strangely defensive. "Do you really think I'm like that?"

"I don't think you're purposefully rude. I think you have little patience for history and ceremony and rituals, and so you may be inclined not to take them seriously, which could potentially offend people who do."

He thought about that for a minute. "If people are offended by something so trivial, then there's nothing I can do about that."

"But a lot of people don't think it's trivial at all."

"What's not trivial?"

"History. Tradition. Things that have been passed down for generations. There's meaning in all those things. Meaning that gives a lot of people their identity. If you say their traditions are trivial, you're implying their identities are trivial too. That seems pretty narrow to me, if you want to know the truth."

He frowned, feeling like she hadn't quite understood his point of view. "It's not about their identities. It's about trivial rituals that serve no purpose."

"Afternoon tea serves a purpose though. It's a way of building community that has been formed and sustained for a really long time. Community is important. There's a real purpose."

"But you can just as easily form community at the kitchen table. You don't need a crystal pitcher."

"But it makes the guests feel important. It's a gesture of grace."

"It doesn't make me feel important."

"Yeah, I wouldn't think so." Her words were perfectly polite, as always, but the tone seemed almost snide underlying it.

He searched her face, looking for a sign of what she was thinking. Whatever it was, it wasn't flattering toward him.

She glanced away when she saw him peering at her. "Anyway," she said, "for someone who doesn't believe in traditions, it's pretty ironic that you own the Claremont. Isn't that whole place supposed to be the epitome of Southern grace and elegance?"

"Of course. Just because I don't care for them myself doesn't mean I can't recognize that others do and use it to my advantage. That's what the entire hospitality industry is about."

"I guess. But it seems strange that you can put them into action so well in the hotel and not really believe in any of that. I mean, Cyrus Damon has been so successful with all the Damon properties because he really believes in what they stand for. Maybe you really do too, deep down. After all, you're going through this whole marriage as a gesture toward your mother because of her attachment to history. That means something, doesn't it?"

"Don't be hoping in that direction. I have no soul of tradition behind my practical exterior. I love my mom, and I'm doing it because she wants it. But the marriage is as fake as all the rituals of the Claremont. Faking it is easy. That's all I know how to do."

She was eying him out of the corner of her eye as they carried the tea back to the garden. "You seem to care a lot about things being easy."

He stiffened at the implications. "What's that supposed to mean?"

"Nothing. Just that you say 'easy' a lot, and it seems to be the guiding force of your decision-making. The fake marriage was easier than trying to be honest with Gina, so you did it. Faking other people's traditions is easier than establishing some of your own, so that's what you do. Don't you ever do things that are hard?"

He was torn between feeling known—like she had seen into the heart of him—and being offended since she didn't seem to appreciate what she'd found. "Not if I can help it. Why should you do things the hard way if there are easier ways available?"

"Maybe the hard way is better."

"Not if they both reach the same end."

"Maybe the hard way is the only way to get what you really want."

"I haven't found that to be the case."

She was shaking her head, but she didn't look judgmental or annoyed. She looked slightly amused and still interested. "Maybe that's because you've never quite figured out what you really want."

He didn't know what to say to that, but they'd rejoined the old ladies anyway, so he didn't have a chance to reply at all.

~

Charleston wasn't at all what Deanna was expecting.

She'd really been looking forward to the trip. She and Mitchell had been getting along well for the past week. She knew he had to do some work, but she figured there would still be time for them to do a little sightseeing and enjoy the city. Otherwise, why had she been invited along at all?

But things didn't work out the way she'd been hoping.

The trip was fine since they flew first-class, which was more comfortable than any of her previous flying experiences. Mitchell wasn't real chatty, but he was polite, and he kind of looked out for her as they were in the airport and taxis, taking care of her luggage and making sure she was always at his side.

She liked that about him and liked that it seemed to be unconscious—just something he did naturally.

He'd reserved them a two-bedroom suite, which he must have paid a fortune for, but it was a relief because it would mean sex wouldn't always be an unspoken question between them. It was just midday when they got into their suite, so she hoped they might do something for the rest of the day.

Instead, he set up his computer and got on the phone even before he'd put his luggage into his room.

Evidently, he wanted to get right to work.

She shrugged it off and went into her room to shower and rest. When he was still working when she came back out, she said she was going to walk around outside.

She enjoyed her stroll, stopping in shops and taking pictures of the lovely architecture and several beautiful gardens. So she was in a good mood when she returned and was resolved to enjoy the trip.

Mitchell went out to dinner with her that first night, and they both seemed to have a good time. But the next morning she slept in, and he was gone when she woke up.

He was thinking of investing in a hotel here, and he had a series of meetings lined up to explore the possibility. She hadn't realized they'd start before breakfast though.

He was gone all day, so she had to amuse herself, taking a taxi to several of the normal historical spots and taking the ferry out to the fort. He called her once to make sure she was okay, but he sounded busy and distracted, so she didn't talk very long. He asked her to have dinner with him that evening, which she was happy about—until she realized it was a business dinner and she was just there as an accessory.

So she went to bed tired and disappointed on the second night but still hopeful that the next day would be better.

On the third and final day, she was genuinely annoyed. He acted like having her come was a nice gesture and a way for them to establish a workable marriage. But it had obviously just been an empty gesture since he must have known he wouldn't have time for her.

She might as well have taken the trip by herself.

She didn't even go out that afternoon since she was so tired and depressed by the whole thing.

It should teach her a lesson though. She didn't have to look at Mitchell as the enemy, but she couldn't rely on him too much. She knew that much about him now.

He wasn't a bad guy—not at all—but if there was an easy road to take, he would take it.

Even if it wasn't the road she wanted to take.

She was telling herself she had no right to be angry about it. She'd had no reason to expect anything different. And she'd mostly succeeded in her mental pep talk, so she was able to smile at him sincerely when he finally returned at about seven in the evening.

He'd said he'd be back before five, but she hadn't expected him to be on time since he hadn't on any of the previous days.

She was sitting on the floor, leaning against the couch in the sitting room of the suite and working on a pair of earrings with the small container of beads she'd brought with her.

"How did everything go?" she asked in a perfectly friendly tone.

He gave a grunt and collapsed on the couch.

She looked up at him, noting that his face was tired and his eyes were kind of clouded. "Not good?" she prompted.

He grunted again.

"What does that mean?"

He gave a half shrug. "It was fine. I'm not sure how it will turn out yet."

"Then why do you look so depressed?"

He frowned at her. "I'm not depressed."

"Okay." She was really starting to get annoyed now. Couldn't he even be friendly, after abandoning her to herself for three days to do business? "Then why do you not look happy about things? I thought you said things looked promising yesterday."

He had said that, briefly and without any details. But it was a better conversation than they were having today.

"I'm not sure how things look. I need to do some more work."

"Ah." She looked back at the earring she was working on, sliding tiny beads onto a fine wire loop. No wonder he looked frustrated. He liked things to be easy and quick, and this situation must not be either.

"What does that mean?"

"What does *what* mean?"

"Ah," he said, mimicking her tone earlier. "What did that mean?"

"It meant, oh, I understand. What do you think it means?" Her tone was a bit sharp since his had been too.

"What do you understand?"

"That you're upset that things aren't going easily. Why are you in such a bad mood?"

"Why do you assume I get upset every time things don't go easily?"

She gave a surprised huff. "Because you obviously do. I know you well enough by now to at least know that. Are you really going to deny it?"

"I'm going to deny that you know me as well as you think when all you do is make unkind assumptions about me."

She almost choked on her indignation. "What the hell are you talking about? I've been nothing but patient for the past few days even though you haven't been making it easy."

"What did I do now?"

"You didn't do anything. Absolutely nothing. Just drag me with you to Charleston with the idea that it will be a fun trip that will make it easier for us to get along when you really just plan to abandon me on my own for three straight days."

"I had to work. Did you think I would ignore the work I was here to do in order to entertain you?"

"I didn't think anything!" Her voice was too loud, but his was too. Both of them were trembling with anger, glaring at each other heatedly. "I never asked for you to entertain me. I haven't complained once the whole time we've been here even though you said this would be like a honeymoon, which would be hard when we are barely ever in the same room."

"You've made it perfectly clear you don't want to be in the same room as me."

She gasped. "The *bedroom*. Not every other room in the city. Do you think it was fun for me to have to do everything alone?"

"I could have arranged for someone to—"

"I didn't want you to arrange some tour guide for me."

"Then what did you want?"

She'd wanted him to do a few things with her, but that was obviously too much to hope for. Too much to even hope he'd recognize it. "I don't want anything from you," she snapped, turning around and deciding she might as well go to her room. Otherwise, she might do something silly like scratch the skin off his face.

He reached out to grab her arm, turning her around to face him again. "What do you want from me?" he demanded again. "How the hell am I supposed to know unless you tell me?"

"Any normal person would have known without being told," she said, "but I shouldn't have expected that from you."

He seemed taken aback by the words, and she was troubled when she heard her own words. Despite her intense irritation, she cleared her throat. "Sorry. That was too mean. I shouldn't have said that. I just meant—"

She never got a chance to tell him what she meant because he suddenly pulled her toward him and started kissing her.

SIX

Mitchell had never felt like this in his life.

It was like he was possessed—like some sort of animalistic force had taken possession of his body. He'd been fighting against lust for Deanna for the past two weeks, ever since that painfully frustrating wedding night. When they'd arrived in Charleston, it had gotten even worse since the romantic setting and the intimate nature of the suite made it hard for him to think of anything but sex.

So he'd made up reasons to stay away from her so he wouldn't make a fool of himself by coming on to her again, when it was clear she didn't want him.

This was the last straw though. She was standing in front of him, wearing nothing but little pajamas that clung to her hips and breasts, and she was flushed and panting with passion.

His body couldn't recognize that the passion was anger. It could only roar in his head that this was what he wanted. *She* was what he wanted.

So he stupidly—without premeditation—reached out to grab and kiss her. If he'd been able to think, he probably would have assumed she'd pull back and slap his face.

She'd told him very plainly that she didn't want to have sex with him.

But she didn't pull back. After a moment of freezing with what felt like surprise, she made a little sound in the back of her throat and reached around to cling to his neck with her arms, her entire body responding to his kiss.

Pleasure and satisfaction now roared in his head with the hunger, and he pulled her more tightly against him, wanting to feel all of her pressed against his body. His eyes blurred and his ears buzzed and his groin throbbed as he plunged into her mouth with his tongue.

She was soft and warm and willing, and he couldn't get enough.

When the kiss finally broke, he still couldn't pull away. He pressed little kisses across her face and jaw as she panted desperately.

"What is happening?" she whispered, as if she were just as possessed by this force as he was.

"I don't know," he admitted, sliding his hands down to cup her bottom and lifting her as she wrapped her legs around his middle. "But I don't want it to stop."

She kept trying to kiss him as he carried her into his bedroom, his body one tight, coiled ache.

He laid her down on the bed, staring down at her lush, sprawled body, the way her dark hair spread out around her face, the way the flush of her cheeks tapered off into the paleness of her neck, the way her tight nipples were visible beneath the fabric of her camisole.

And every detail stoked his desire even more.

With a guttural sound, he moved over her, kissing her deeply as she moved restlessly beneath him, stroking his back, trying to wrap one of her legs around his thigh.

"Mitchell," she gasped, when he lowered his face to take one breast in his mouth. "I don't know what's happening to me. I feel…" She cried out when he tweaked her nipple with his teeth. "Out of control."

He was deeply relieved to hear he wasn't alone in this. He couldn't stop touching her. Couldn't keep from pressing his pelvis into her with helpless little pushes.

"Just go with it," he murmured. "It's too good to stop." He slid down her pajama pants so he could see her whole body, and his spirit howled with satisfaction at the sight of her lovely naked flesh.

She was panting frantically as she pulled his shirttails out of his trousers, so he paused to help her get rid of his clothes. Then both of them were naked, and they were kissing again, and nothing had ever felt nearly so good.

"Oh, please," she gasped, her voice right at his ear as he mouthed the pulse in her throat. "I can't wait anymore, Mitchell. Please."

He couldn't wait anymore either. He pulled up, giving his aching erection a quick squeeze as he tried to think clearly enough to figure out whether they needed a condom.

"I'm not on birth control," she told him, answering his unspoken question.

He'd brought condoms, just in case, so he reached over to the nightstand drawer to grab a packet, unwrapping it with fingers that shook far more than they should.

Then he was rolling it on and positioning himself between her legs, and she was spreading her thighs for him and trying to guide him in.

She was wet and warm and soft, and he moaned helplessly as he entered her. She was tight but pliant, and her whimper sounded like pleasure as she wrapped her arms around him, holding him close.

"Good?" he asked, rather raspingly, when he'd gotten control of the intense surge of need at the feel of being inside her.

"Oh, yeah." She gave a little pump up into him. "Oh, God, it's so good."

It was better than good for him, and he wanted to take her hard—harder than would be comfortable for her. So he reined in the need enough to establish a gentle rhythm, trying to figure out what she liked, what she needed.

She matched his motion initially, settling herself around him. But soon her gasps intensified and, she was bucking up eagerly, trying to speed up their rhythm.

"Faster," she gasped. "I need it faster. Harder."

He responded, taking her faster and harder, letting himself go enough to start building toward climax, the friction needed and pleasing and so good.

"More," she gasped, her face twisting in shameless need. "Oh, God, Mitchell, I need even more."

He made another sound in his throat—this one of intense pleasure since she seemed to want exactly what he wanted to give her. Then he lifted her legs higher so they were wrapped tightly around his waist, and he thrust into her exactly as he wanted.

Her cries of pleasure became louder and more helpless as she surrendered to the sensations, obviously letting go of any restraint or inhibition in a way that fed his need and satisfaction. She was giving all of herself to this— she wanted it so much.

Exactly as he did.

So he let go too, grunting as he built toward climax and then unable to hold it back when it arrived.

The rush of hot pleasure consumed him as he jerked in his final thrusts, greatly relieved when he felt her coming too, crying out as the final moment took her just after him.

They were both gasping and clinging when they came down from the climax, and Mitchell couldn't remember the last time his body and spirit were washed with this kind of satisfaction.

It wasn't merely the normal satiation after a good screw. It felt deeper—like something beyond his libido had been satisfied.

He was lying on top of her, and he must have been too heavy because she started shifting, as if she were uncomfortable.

He rolled over onto his back, pulling her with him. He couldn't seem to let go of her. He had no idea what had gotten into him.

He was never like this.

He even found himself trying to see past her messy hair so he could check her expression. To his relief, she was smiling.

She opened her mouth, like she would say something, but she must have changed her mind. Instead, she nestled against him.

He settled his arm around her and closed his eyes, breathing deeply and enjoying the feeling.

Tomorrow it would change. Tomorrow he'd feel like normal again. Tomorrow he'd likely be annoyed with a wife who was turning out to be anything but easy to manage.

But right now he could just enjoy it. After all, he'd spent his life enjoying each moment without worrying too much about what came afterward.

~

Deanna must have fallen asleep. She hadn't intended to. She thought she would just rest and recover for a minute before she went back to her own bedroom.

But when she opened her eyes, it was dark in the room, and she was still pressed up against Mitchell's body.

The first thing she felt was deep pleasure.

The second thing she felt was deep fear.

She shouldn't be doing this. She'd decided from the very beginning that sex would just complicate things, and she could tell it already had since she was feeling very soft and clinging toward Mitchell now—like she wanted to be close to him, like she wanted him to really like her.

That was stupid since this marriage would only last six months. He'd made it clear from the beginning that he was interested in having sex as a way to pass the time and prevent a long period of imposed celibacy.

It didn't mean anything. It might have been the best sex she'd ever had, but it didn't mean anything to him but a good time.

That meant it couldn't mean anything to her either.

The roiling fear only got stronger as she lay in the dark, so she rolled away from him. His body was generating heat, and all her skin that had been pressed up against him was damp and felt chilled in the cool air of the room.

That didn't matter either though. She just needed to get away.

She was reaching down onto the floor in the hopes of finding her pajamas when an arm came from the other side of the bed and pulled her back.

She gave a squeal of surprise when Mitchell rolled her toward him so she was on her back and he was on top of her.

"What do you think you're doing?" he asked, his voice thick with the kind of texture she'd heard in it before—which she'd already labeled his bedroom voice.

"I was looking for my pajamas. You tossed them over the side somewhere."

"Why do you need your pajamas?" There was enough light in the room to make out his face, and he was smiling down on her.

She couldn't help but smile back. She loved that smile from him—the one that felt real—like it was coming from something genuinely happy inside him and not like he was putting it on to be charming. "I don't normally spend the night naked."

"I don't know why not. It seems like a very good idea to me." He pulled up enough to leer down at her bare breasts with playful exaggeration.

She laughed and tugged up his head by his hair, making him look at her face again. "If men had their choice, then women would never sleep in any clothes at all. And I'm telling you, we'd get cold!"

She still felt that rippling of fear, but it was quickly being drowned out by a lot of other feelings.

He laughed out loud and leaned down to kiss her, and it still felt like he was shaking in amusement as his tongue gently caressed her bottom lip. She tangled her fingers in his thick hair and exhaled as the sensations washed over her.

She'd already made the mistake. It wouldn't matter if the mistake ended with their first round of sex or this one. Might as well enjoy it for as long as she could.

It seemed like an entirely sensible decision to her.

"I can't figure out what it is about you," he murmured against her mouth.

"What can't you figure out?"

"Why I can't keep my hands off you."

"Maybe you're just a victim of your testosterone."

"I don't think so. Because I'm not normally like this."

She couldn't help but like that idea. "You're not normally like *what?*"

"So overcome with lust I can't even see straight."

"Oh." She tried to think of something clever and funny to say even though she was drowning in dangerously soft feelings. "Maybe it's the fact that you're married. Did you always secretly want to be a husband?"

"Uh, no." His mouth was skating down her body now, teasing places that left her squirming with arousal. "I never wanted to be a husband in my life."

Those words gave her a weird, heavy clench that she made herself ignore. "Well, maybe it's the surprise then. Being a husband was so unexpected that your body can't quite make sense of it."

"That must be it." There was laughter in his voice now, even as he nuzzled between her legs. "Might as well indulge it since it won't last very long."

She gasped and parted her thighs for him, choking on the pleasure when she felt his tongue on her intimate flesh.

He pleasured her with his mouth and fingers until she came and then came again. Then he rose up and took her hard, until they were both drenched and exhausted.

Lying together afterward, Deanna couldn't help but think about doing it again.

And then she thought about what he'd said and why he'd said it. He was indulging in a temporary interest—a fleeting desire—knowing it was only temporary.

She had to keep remembering that.

~

When she woke up the next time, it was light in the room, and she knew for sure she'd made a mistake.

She wasn't cuddled up against him now, but she was facing his direction, and as soon as her eyes opened, they landed on him.

He was asleep, lying on his back with the covers pushed down to his waist. One of his arms was hooked up over his head, and he was breathing in slow, deep inhales and exhales.

She watched and listened to him for a while, remembering how he'd acted last night. Not just the passion but the intimacy and laughter.

She'd loved it. All of it. She wanted more of it. She wanted to know him like that more and more, get closer and closer to him.

But that wasn't part of the deal, and she wasn't stupid enough to assume that having sex would change the core of their relationship.

Whatever was between them was temporary, and he had never lied about wanting it to stay that way.

If she didn't pull back immediately, she would end up with a broken heart out of this marriage. She could see it happening already.

It was okay. They could still work things out. She could get out of this thing with her heart intact.

But they couldn't have sex again.

She rolled over to the edge again and reached down for her pajama pants, which she could see in the morning light.

She was pulling them on under the covers when Mitchell opened his eyes.

"Morning," he said, his voice thick with sleep rather than sex.

"Hi." She smiled at him, reaching back to the floor for her camisole.

"It feels too early to be moving yet."

"It's not six yet, but we'll have to get up in a little while anyway. We need to leave before eight to make our flight."

He groaned and closed his eyes.

"You might as well resign yourself to getting up," she said, sounding more awake than she felt since she was clearly more awake than him.

He opened his eyes just a slit and peered at her through them. "We have a little time. I can think of a few ways to resign myself to waking up more pleasantly."

She shook her head, amazed at his appetite since they'd had two fairly vigorous rounds of sex that night. "Not going to happen."

"Are you feeling okay?"

She smiled since his concern sounded sincere. "Yeah, I'm fine. Despite your delusions of grandeur, you're not so huge that it leaves me unable to walk this morning." She made sure her tone was light so he would know she was teasing.

He chuckled and reached out for her, but she stayed out of his reach.

He frowned when she got off the bed. "Where are you going?"

"To my room to get dressed."

"Why are you so standoffish?"

"Because I don't think we should do this again." She tried to sound firm, but she ended up sounding more resigned than anything else, like it was something she didn't really want.

This startled him into sitting up. He rubbed his chin with his hand, making a scratchy sound from his bristles. "Why not? It was fantastic."

She blushed a little at the words, which was ridiculous. "Yeah, it was really good. But I told you before that sex would make things between us more complicated."

"It didn't feel complicated last night."

"Maybe not. But it's starting to feel that way this morning." When it looked like he would argue, she spoke over him. "I'm serious, Mitchell. I know it was good. And I'm sure it would continue to be good. But I... I..." She trailed off, wanting to be honest but not feeling comfortable revealing the deepest parts of her soul to him.

He looked cool and disapproving, but his eyes searched her face. "You want…?"

"I'm not the kind of person who can have sex casually. I just can't. I never have. If I keep having sex with you, I'll eventually want it to mean something, and that means I'll end up getting hurt. I'm not going to do that to myself."

It was all true, and she didn't regret saying it even though it left her feeling naked and strangely young.

Mitchell didn't say anything immediately. He stared at her, clearly processing the words. Several times, it looked like he would start responding, but he never did.

Finally he gave a little nod. "Understood."

She narrowed her eyes. "You're okay with that?"

"What am I supposed to say? That you should keep having sex with me, even if it will hurt you?"

She swallowed hard. "That would be pretty heartless."

"I know. I'm not going to say it. Whatever you think, I'm not entirely heartless."

She sighed. "I don't think you're heartless, Mitchell. I just think you're different from me. I take certain things seriously—like marriage and sex and… and tradition. I know you don't. That's fine. You don't have to. But I hope you understand that I do."

"I do understand. If you want to have sex again, you'll let me know." His eyes smoldered briefly. "I guarantee that I'll keep wanting to have sex with you."

She gulped, feeling a hot flash wash over her.

She would have preferred not to know that. Now she was going to keep wondering if he was thinking about having sex with her, which would make her constantly think about having sex with him.

She felt rattled and a little disappointed as she returned to her bedroom. She was relieved that he'd accepted her decision, but it meant that there was no way—absolutely no way—that he would ever take sex with her seriously.

It clearly hadn't even been a possibility in his mind.

SEVEN

A week later, Mitchell woke up feeling a sense of frustration that was becoming familiar.

Before he'd gotten married, he'd had sex fairly regularly. Whenever he got the itch, it was pretty easy to find some way to scratch it—usually a one-night stand since more serious relationships were too much hassle. But on a daily basis, the desire to have sex had never particularly troubled him.

It did now.

He woke up thinking about Deanna, and he went to bed thinking about Deanna, and in the middle of the day, just sitting in his office, he would find himself thinking about her too. Imagining having sex with her again—in any number of creative ways and locations.

It was absolutely ridiculous.

He was starting to realize it had been a mistake to have sex last week in Charleston, no matter how good it had been, since it had merely whetted his appetite, and now he wanted her even more than he had before.

He tried to push the thought of her to the back of his mind. It was a normal day, after all. He had to work out. Then go to the Claremont and do his job. He had a few important phone calls in the afternoon. Then he and Deanna were scheduled to go to the ballet this evening as his weekly public function.

He was pretty sure she was going to make him go to church on Sunday for hers.

So he roused himself from bed, scattered the erotic thoughts that kept pestering him, and pulled on his workout clothes.

On his way to the basement, he heard a strange noise from the library, so he stuck his head in to see what was going on.

It was Deanna. She leaning over, evidently trying to move a table across the room. It was made of heavy wood, and she was tiny, so she was obviously having to work hard at it.

She still wore her pajamas—her normal ensemble of soft cotton pants and thin camisole—and he could see the outline of her underwear through the fabric since it was stretched across her rounded ass.

His body immediately took interest, but his mind was, for the moment, the stronger force. "What the hell are you doing?"

She was so startled she jumped, releasing the table and whirling around. "You scared me."

"Sorry," he said, not particularly apologetic. "What are you doing?"

"I was just moving the table over to the window where there's more light. Is that okay?" She wiped her forehead with the back of her hand and pushed one lacy strap back in place. "You said I could make myself at home."

It looked like she was worried he'd be mad at her, which was very annoying. Surely she didn't think he was so demanding and uptight. "It's fine. You can do whatever you like. By why are you doing it all by yourself?"

"I didn't want to bother you. I'm used to doing things by myself."

He sighed and shook his head, walking over to grab the sides of the table.

She ran around to the other side, and together they moved the table where she wanted it.

"It's getting too cluttered to do my beads in my little sitting room, so I thought I'd do them here if that's all right. You never seem to use this room much."

"I don't use it at all. Just grab a book occasionally. You can completely change it if you want to set it up differently. I can get new furniture if you need—"

"No, no." She interrupted him, giving him a little smile he really liked, as if she were pleased and appreciative. "It's just fine as it is. I only wanted to move the table by the window. Thank you so much."

"You don't have to keep thanking me. This is your home as much as mine—for the next five months and one week." He added the last phrase to remind himself since he kept forgetting the end date wasn't that far away.

"Do you need some help bringing down all your beads?" he asked, troubled by the line of his thoughts.

"No, I can get them." When she saw his cool glare, she laughed sheepishly. "Okay. If you don't mind. Thank you."

She was beaming at him as they went up to collect all her paraphernalia, and her smile made him feel foolishly proud of himself even though he'd done almost nothing to be proud of except behave like a decent human being.

She was telling him where to put the tins of beads back in the library when he noticed one particular container with a clear lid that had a variety of beads that all seemed distinct and eye-catching. "What are these for?" he asked, gesturing toward the container. "I haven't seen any of these on the stuff you make."

"No, those are all my favorites. Whenever I see any that I particularly like, I put them in there."

"But you don't use them?"

"No. It's silly, I guess, but I keep saving them up. I have this idea of making them all into some sort of wall hanging or something."

"Why don't you?" He could picture them all together and thought it would make a really impressive piece of art.

"It would take forever, and then it would be so expensive no one would buy it."

"They probably would."

"Well, I wouldn't want to sell it."

"Then just do it for yourself."

She gave a little shrug. "I'd never do something that took so long just to keep it. I love doing my beads, but can only justify it because it has the potential to earn a little money. It would just feel self-indulgent to do it all for myself."

He gazed at her for a minute, thinking she was so pretty and intelligent and practical and self-sufficient, and he wondered how many chances she'd had in her life to do something just for the sheer pleasure of it, something to please only her.

He'd spent most of his life doing just that.

"What's the matter?" she asked, looking at him curiously.

He was feeling strangely close to her, and he wanted to stay to talk some more, dig into her soul. But the thought made him nervous, so he thought it was better to make himself scarce.

"I'd better work out while I have the time," he muttered.

"Sure," she said with a smile that was just a little wistful. "Thanks so much for your help."

He wondered if it was his imagination or if she was disappointed that he'd left so abruptly.

He almost hoped she was.

~

A couple of days later, they were sitting together in the library after dinner.

Deanna had come into the room to work on her beads, and he'd ended up following her since it felt strangely lonely to hang about by himself.

He'd never felt lonely in his own house before. He assumed it was just a passing feeling.

He'd acted like he'd come into the room to read, but instead he ended up sitting across the table from her, pretending to help her with the earrings she was making.

Deanna giggled as she watched him try to get the tiny beads on the wire.

"There's no reason to laugh," he said with a playfully disapproving look. "My fingers are a lot bigger than yours."

"I know. You're doing just fine." Her face was smiling and affectionate and so pretty it took his breath away.

"Which one goes next?" he asked, gesturing to the beads she'd pulled out for the piece of jewelry.

"You can choose the order. What do you think would look nice?"

"I have no idea." He eyed the silver and turquoise beads warily. "I guess we should alternate the colors?"

"That's what I was thinking." She was already finished with the matching earring she'd been making, and she showed him how she'd looped up the wire and fastened on the closure. "These are pretty simple."

"They don't look simple to me." Mitchell focused on getting the beads strung without dropping them, and after a few minutes he looked up to see she was still watching him with a fond smile. "I don't think beads are my thing," he said.

She chuckled. "I wouldn't have thought so."

"That's a lot of work. Who'd have thought it would take so long to make something so little?"

"But they're pretty." She'd finished off his earring and was looking with genuine pleasure down at the matching pair. "It's worth the work to end up with something so pretty."

"It's not worth it to me."

Her expression changed slightly as she raised her eyes to meet his, but he didn't know what she was thinking.

"Did you ever help your mom cook when you were a kid?" she asked.

She'd changed the subject so quickly he thought he might have missed something. "Yeah. Sometimes."

"Cooking is similar. It's sometimes tedious and a lot of work, but it's worth it after it's done. What did you make with your mom besides pancakes?"

He'd already told her about the nights his mom had come home from work late and they'd make pancakes, and it was nice that she'd remembered it. "Cookies and cake. I mostly helped so I could lick the bowls. I never cared much about helping with the bigger meals." He thought back to himself as a kid. "I guess even then I didn't want to work too hard."

The last words were soft, spoken almost to himself. It was like he'd suddenly seen himself from a distance and didn't really like what he saw.

"Is that why you're not into serious relationships?" She'd cut a new piece of wire and was staring down at it, the question asked almost diffidently.

"Yeah. I guess. I don't know."

Her eyes lifted. "You don't know, or you don't want to tell me?"

He wasn't even sure of the answer to that question.

"When was the last time you really tried to have a serious relationship with a woman?"

He thought back. He'd had nothing but one-night stands and temporary flings for years. *Years*. "In grad school, I guess."

Deanna looked genuinely interested even though her hands never stopped working. "Who was that?"

"Her name was Heather. She was in one of my classes. I was totally hung up on her." He hadn't thought about the woman for ages, and the memory was almost surprising.

"Did you ask her out?"

"Yeah. We went out a few times since we both believed in just having a good time. But then my cousin was getting married, and I invited her to the wedding."

"She said no?"

Mitchell's chest felt unusually tight, more from admitting this to Deanna than the memory itself. "Yeah. She just wanted to have a good time, and she was mad at me for changing terms."

"Were you heartbroken?" Deanna asked, almost breathlessly.

He was afraid she might be blowing the story out of proportion. It wasn't some sort of deep secret to his soul. It was just a random thing that happened. "I don't know. I was disappointed and then I was angry. I was…" He cleared his throat. "I was mean to her."

Deanna's brow lowered. "Why were you mean to her?"

He gave a little shrug. "That's just what I do when I put myself out there and am rejected." He sighed. "It's a way of dealing with it. I guess I've always been like that."

"That's not unusual. If you feel like you're being attacked, it's human nature to strike back. Not that poor Heather deserved it." Deanna's eyes were searching his face. "What's the matter? What are you thinking about now?"

He had absolutely no reason to answer her, but he found himself doing it anyway. "I was just thinking back to when I was eight. I wanted to meet my father."

Her expression changed. "I thought you said he was a salesman passing through town."

"He was. I never got to meet him. I wanted my mom to tell me his name so I could contact him. I pestered my poor mom for weeks about it, and she kept putting me off. Finally she admitted that she'd contacted him several times over the years to see if he'd changed his mind, but he still didn't want to know me."

His voice cracked slightly on the last words, and for the first time in a really long time, he once again felt the wave of crushing rejection he'd felt as a boy, when he'd wanted so much to be loved by a father only to hear that he wasn't wanted at all.

Deanna was silent for several moments. "I'm sorry," she murmured at last. "That's... that must have really hurt."

"It did." He shook his head to dispel the mood. "Not now, but it was hard to take when I was eight. I was so angry. I wrote my dad a searing letter of contempt and outrage, and I put it in an envelope for my mom to mail to him."

"Did she do it?"

"I doubt it, but it made me feel better to think she did." He let out his breath, wishing he hadn't admitted something so vulnerable to Deanna. He wanted her to think he was impressive, not some silly, spiteful, lazy boy.

Her expression didn't look surprised or disappointed in him. In fact, she still looked rather soft. "It's nice that you're close to your mom."

He should have kept his mouth shut, but instead he admitted, "I wasn't always."

"Really?"

"Yeah. In college and then through my twenties, I was... I don't know, I was kind of distant. She always called me, but I never made much effort toward her. Same with Brie, to tell you the truth."

Deanna believed in family. She was really close to her own. She wasn't going to like knowing that he'd been such a bad son and brother.

"Well," she said softly, "at least you're close to both of them now. Does Brie have a different father?"

"Yeah. Another loser. My mom always had bad taste in men. But at least Brie knows who he is, and she occasionally gets to see him. He lives in Savannah too."

"Oh. I guess maybe that's why you don't believe in marriage, since you never saw a good one."

He was starting to feel a little uncomfortable, so he turned the conversation intentionally. "Did you?"

"Yeah. My parents had a good marriage, and I was eleven when they died, so I was old enough to really see their marriage."

"They were in a car accident?"

"Yeah."

"Eleven is pretty young to lose both of your parents." He could just picture her as a girl, with her long hair and big eyes, trying desperately to be grown-up enough to take care of her family.

She was staring down at her beadwork. "Our grandmother stepped up to take care of us. She's... she's eccentric, but she loves us."

"She doesn't act like she loves you." He said the words before he could think through whether they were wise.

Deanna didn't look offended. "I know, but she does. She's still trapped in the past in a lot of ways, and what she thinks is best for us isn't always the best. But she tries. She might not be warm and fuzzy, but people love in different ways."

"Still, it seems like you've had to sacrifice a lot to help take care of your family. Did you never want to go to college?

111

Surely you could have gotten grants or scholarships or something if you couldn't afford it."

She put down her beads. "Yeah. I could have. But I never really felt the strong desire to go to college—not like Kelly has. It seemed more important for me to work full-time so I could make a real salary as soon as possible. Maybe it was stupid." She closed her eyes. "Maybe I've made nothing but stupid decisions."

"I didn't mean to imply that," he said quickly, worried because she looked suddenly glum. "I was just asking."

She opened her eyes to meet his squarely. "But you think I've been kind of weak, don't you?"

He didn't think she was weak anymore. Not even close. But there was something serious to what she was asking, so he answered her carefully. "I don't think you're weak. I think maybe you've poured yourself so much into doing what you think is good for your family that you don't always think about what's really good for you."

She broke their gaze and looked at a spot in the air just past his shoulder. After a minute, she gave a little nod, as if she might have admitted to herself that he was right. She finally said, "You know, Harrison Damon said something similar—about making sure family loyalty doesn't lead you into something that's wrong. It's... interesting to think about."

Mitchell didn't think what Damon had said was the same thing he was trying to say.

And he didn't appreciate having Damon dragged into a private conversation between him and his wife.

All he said, however, was, "Hmm."

~

A few weeks later, Mitchell was actually looking forward to getting home after work.

He'd never been someone like that—someone who longed for the end of the day so he could leave work—but the feeling had gradually been developing over the past weeks.

He and Deanna had started having dinner together most nights. Sometimes she would have been fixing it as he got home, and sometimes they'd fix it together. And then they'd hang out and watch movies or work out, or she'd tease him into helping with her beads.

He was still almost crippled by lust sometimes and usually went to bed physically frustrated—unless he gave in and took a shower to take care of it—but his evenings were becoming very enjoyable nonetheless.

It was an entirely new feeling—to look forward to something so... quiet.

But he was eager to get home as he left the Claremont just before six on a Thursday evening. He wondered if Deanna had any plans for dinner tonight. He wondered what she was doing. What kind of mood she was in.

He wondered if there was a way he could convince her that sex wasn't as off the table between them as she seemed to think.

He was generally in a good mood as he entered the house. He paused, glancing around, looking for a sign as to where Deanna might be. She was usually in the library or outside on the patio at this time of day or in the kitchen working on dinner, but she wasn't any of those places.

He wandered around until her suite was the only remaining place in the house for her to be. He tapped on the door since it was closed.

"Yeah," she called out, her voice sounding rather distracted.

He walked in and found her on the floor, leaning against the big chair instead of sitting on it. In her lap was the laptop he'd bought her last week when her old one had died.

"What's the matter?" he asked, immediately concerned by her expression. She was staring at the screen.

She glanced up at him and then back at the screen, her features twisting. "What? Oh, it's nothing."

He walked over and lowered himself to sit beside her. "Well, it's obviously something. You're upset."

"It's just…" She cleared her throat. "A friend sent me this link to a blog. It's some sort of local news blog for Savannah, although it looks like mostly gossip to me. Anyway, there's a story about us. I mean, about you. And me."

His forehead wrinkled, and he took the laptop from her hands so he could read the screen. The story was indeed about them—about their marriage—including a lot of speculation about how he seemed to have "bought" her as a bride.

"Shit," he muttered. "What the hell?"

"I guess it's because we started working on the house, and they must know the Beauforts wouldn't have money to fund it unless you were giving us the money. I don't understand why anyone cares about our marriage though."

"They'll care about anything that's not their business." He was angry—surprisingly angry since it was just silly gossip on a not-very-popular blog—but he didn't like the way the article was talking about Deanna as bought and paid for, implying she was some sort of prostitute.

He didn't like it at all.

He grew even angrier when he looked at her again and saw the tension of emotion on her face.

"I'm sorry," he murmured, lifting a hand to cup her face without thinking. "Are you really upset?"

"A little. The insinuations are insulting." She looked slightly surprised. "Mostly I thought you'd be upset."

He lifted his eyebrows. "I don't give a damn. People have always said anything they want about me. It doesn't bother me at all. I don't care about that kind of thing, remember?" He gave a half smile that he hoped would make her smile too.

It did. Her face relaxed for a moment as she smiled back. But then she said, "But what about Gina? The Darlington Café deal hasn't gone through yet, has it?"

He bit back a curse, suddenly remembering that not unimportant detail. "No. Not until next month. It probably won't be an issue though. I doubt she reads that blog, and we can always shrug it off as malicious gossip."

She was frowning again as she scanned over the story. "Do you think we should act more like a normal couple? No one knows we don't share a bedroom, but out in public, I mean."

"I think we act mostly like a normal couple when we go out. Most couples aren't all over each other in public, so it's not like we're totally unusual."

"I know. But we just go to public functions. Most couples go out to eat or on outings, just the two of them. The article says we're never seen on dates."

He made an impatient noise in his throat and reached over to close out the browser. "Just forget about that stupid story. It's not important enough for us to worry about."

"Okay." She stared at her laptop screen even though the story was no longer visible.

He sighed. "You're still upset."

"I'm not. I just want to make sure we do everything we need to do—I mean, for the marriage to be convincing. We're getting our whole house rebuilt, so I want to make sure you're... you're..."

"I'm what?" For some reason, his breath caught in his throat and his pulse sped up.

"You're getting everything you need from this marriage, that I'm holding up my side of the bargain."

She was serious. She genuinely had no idea how much he was enjoying being married to her, spending time with her, even though it wasn't involving sex.

She had absolutely no idea.

He felt a little awkward about telling her since the feeling was so new and uncomfortable, and he was pretty sure he'd end up sounding stupid and trite.

"It's fine," he ended up saying gruffly. "Everything is fine."

Her eyes flew up to his face. "Are you sure?"

"Of course. I have no complaints about the marriage." He cleared his throat and managed a leering expression. "Although I still wouldn't say no to sex."

She giggled, looking remarkably pretty and vulnerable somehow. "Sorry. I'm sure it can't be comfortable to have to refrain for so long."

"Are you saying it's comfortable for you?" He didn't at all like the idea that she wasn't at least a little bit interested in sex with him.

"I've gone without sex for six months plenty of times in my life."

"Really?"

She shook her head. "I think you're dramatically overestimating my social life. I've had two serious boyfriends in my life—none of the relationships lasting more than a year. And I only have sex with guys I'm serious about, so..."

He thought about that, thinking through what it told him about her. "You had sex with me," he said at last.

She blushed visibly and glanced away. "That was an accident."

He burst into laughter and reached over to wrap an arm around her, pulling her into a quick half hug. "Anytime you'd like another slipup like that, just let me know. I promise I'll be available for an accident of my own."

She was laughing too when she pulled away.

Hit with a spontaneous idea, he suggested, "Do you want to go out tonight? Just the two of us?"

She straightened up, looking surprised again. "Sure. That's a good idea. That would help dispel the idea that we're not a normal couple."

For some reason, Mitchell felt a drop in his chest at her words. He hadn't suggested it to stop the rumors.

He'd suggested it because he thought she would enjoy it.

~

After the shock of seeing the story on their marriage, Deanna had a really good evening.

A *really* good evening.

So good that it made her very nervous.

She and Mitchell both showered and changed before they went out, so she felt fresh and pretty in a new blue sundress. They went to a nice low-key restaurant in the historic downtown area, and then they walked through some of the neighborhoods, looking at houses and gardens, stopping at little shops, and later getting ice cream.

Mitchell held her hand as they walked—she assumed so they could convey the appropriate romantic vibe should anyone recognize them—but it felt really nice, and she wasn't at all tempted to pull away from him.

As the evening progressed and they were strolling in companionable silence, Deanna started to get nervous.

She shouldn't be enjoying it so much. She shouldn't be thinking about this as natural. She shouldn't be wanting it to continue, deepen.

They were already more than two months into their six-month marriage, and the end date was looming large.

Mitchell seemed to be having a good time with her, but that was his nature. He enjoyed himself. He took the easiest route. He rode out whatever wave was in front of him at the moment, and then he moved on as soon as it passed.

He'd admitted it openly over and over again.

She couldn't invest in this relationship emotionally because she knew he would never do so himself.

If she wasn't careful, she was going to get hurt.

Really hurt before this thing was over.

The reflections put a damper on her mood as they approached an ornate fountain. Very gently, she pulled her hand away from his since it was feeling far too nice held in his warm, strong grip.

She fussed with her hair for a minute as an excuse to pull her hand away, and then she just didn't offer it back.

She stood for a moment, staring at the water gush out of a dolphin's mouth in the fountain, wishing faintly that she could let go to that extent, just let everything pour out, regardless of consequences.

She couldn't though. She was too smart. She was too careful. She'd lived her life desperately trying to hold together the edges of her world since it always felt on the verge of falling apart, and she couldn't just release it because she wanted for once to enjoy the freedom.

She'd regret it tomorrow. And the next day. And so many days to come.

Mitchell had paused with her, also looking at the fountain, and he reached over almost unconsciously to take her hand again.

She pulled it away before he could reach it.

She wasn't looking at him, but she felt him frown and reach for her again.

She ended up—very stupidly—hiding her hand behind her back.

"What the hell?" he muttered, putting his hands on her shoulders and turning her to face him.

"Sorry," she said, feeling silly and so young. "My hand was getting hot."

"No, it wasn't." He was searching her face intently. "What's the matter? You were having a good time, and now you're upset about something."

"It's nothing."

"Don't lie to me."

His voice was so intimate, almost entitled, that it frightened her and angered her at the same time. "I can lie to you if I want."

"But why would you?"

"Because maybe there are certain things you don't need to know."

"Maybe I want to know them."

"Maybe it doesn't always matter what you want."

It was a ridiculous argument, and they both seemed to recognize it at the same time. They both smiled and relaxed, and Mitchell pulled her into a soft hug she just didn't have the strength to pull away from.

"What were you worrying about?" he asked after a minute, his mouth against her ear.

"Nothing. Everything. I don't know."

He drew back enough to look down into her face. "I wish you wouldn't worry all the time."

"I have to worry."

"Why?"

She had no idea why she was admitting the truth so openly, but she did. "If I don't, it feels like everything will fall apart."

"What will?"

"Everything. My whole life."

"But what if it doesn't?"

"But what if it does?"

"You can't control that anyway, so why drag yourself down by worrying about things you can't control?"

"But some things I *can* control. And it's important to me to make good decisions in the things I can control."

"Maybe it should be important to you to let yourself enjoy life more each day even if things aren't perfect the following day."

"I enjoy life plenty."

"Do you?" He was still gazing down at her, and it felt like he was seeing her for real, completely—like she was the only thing in the world he was seeing. "I'm not sure you do. You never just let yourself go."

"That's because letting yourself go means you make bad decisions."

"Not all the time—unless every one of your instincts is bad."

"They are. All my instincts are bad."

He chuckled. "No, they're not." He leaned down to press a soft kiss on her lips. "I promise you—your instincts aren't all bad."

Her heart and mind and body all felt like they were soaring, and she couldn't help but reach up to wind her arms around his neck. "Some of them are bad," she murmured, her voice surprisingly husky. "Some of them are very, very bad."

He chuckled as he kissed her again, the amusement soft and warm and delicious as it vibrated through her body. "But see, those instincts are actually the best ones."

Her whole body softened against him, and she opened her lips to his tongue, and as the kiss deepened, her existence seemed entirely overwhelmed with pure pleasure.

His hands had slid down to her hips, and he was pressing her against his groin, and she loved the shameless entitlement of it, as if he was allowed to touch her, move her, exactly as he wanted.

But it was all feeling so good and free and intensely dangerous that a jolt of panic rushed through her and she clumsily pulled away.

He groaned as he reluctantly released her.

"We agreed to no kissing," she gasped, hugging her arms to her chest, desperately wanting to grab and kiss him again.

He rubbed his face with his hands, clearly disappointed and frustrated. "I never agreed to no kissing."

"But we agreed to no sex."

"I told you that you could change your mind at any point."

"I don't want to change my mind."

He was shaking his head. "Yes, you do."

"Well, not all of me wants to change my mind."

"You do want to change your mind. You're just worried about tomorrow. You don't understand that it's right now that really matters."

"Tomorrow matters to me too," she said, meaning every word. "I'm really sorry."

He breathed heavily for a moment until he finally released the tension with a resigned look. "Okay. It's up to you."

It was very nice of him to respect her wishes. In fact, she'd resent the hell out of him if he pressed on even after she'd said no. But part of her wished he would sweep her off her feet so she wouldn't have to think and worry and predict disaster. So she could just enjoy the moment, the way he could.

Even though, in her heart of hearts, she knew disaster would be coming. She would never be able to be with him for just the moment. She wasn't built that way. If she let herself go and gave herself to him again, she'd be giving all of herself to him, she'd be letting herself fall.

And she'd be crushed at the end of the fall when he wasn't there to catch her.

He wouldn't be. He'd never been anything but honest about that. When six months was up, he would move on to the next thing that was easy and enjoyable.

And no matter how hard it was to resist him right now, it would be harder to watch him walk away, after she'd fallen in love with him.

EIGHT

A few weeks later was the wedding of Mandy Milton and Benjamin Damon, and Mitchell and Deanna were sitting together in a stiff wooden pew of a historic church in Savannah.

It was still twenty-five minutes before the wedding would begin, but the church was already packed. Deanna was glad she'd hurried Mitchell up and made sure they arrived early.

Mitchell looked handsome and respectable in a gray suit, although his hair was a little too long and wasn't lying quite right. He looked familiar, known, like she could close her eyes and still see exactly what his expression would be at any given moment.

Like a really good friend. Or family.

He also looked so sexy she had trouble not touching him, but she was used to that.

"Where did all these people come from?" Mitchell murmured in her ear. "Don't Ben and Mandy live in California?"

"Yeah. But he grew up here, and I guess Mandy has tons of friends. She seemed really friendly and social the few times I've met her."

Deanna grinned when she saw Harrison, stunningly handsome and immanently respectable in his tux, walk up the aisle after guiding someone to her seat. His face didn't break a smile when his eyes landed on her, but he gave her a discreet wink.

She hid a laugh and caught a glimpse of Mitchell frowning.

"Are you still annoyed with Harrison for helping me out with the contract?"

"I'm not annoyed with him for helping you out," he muttered. "I'd be annoyed with any man who winked at my wife that way."

She tried to repress the laughter. "Don't be ridiculous. He's evidently like the most devoted husband in the history of the world. That's his wife over there." She nodded toward a blond woman near the front of the church—as freshly pretty and vibrant as a wildflower—who was holding an infant in a lovely white dress.

"I was talking to Mandy on Thursday at the shower, and she was telling me about how Harrison and Marietta got together. It's so romantic. Harrison climbed a mountain for her. And then they had to try so hard to have a baby." Deanna sighed. "He's a great husband."

She was just being conversational since the stories Mandy had told her were so interesting, but she felt a little wistful at the end, thinking of what it must be like to have a husband so devoted, so completely in love, that he'd do the hardest things for her.

Mitchell was great. He was amazing. But he wasn't devoted to her, and he would always take the easiest road.

"Well, he's not *your* husband," Mitchell said, sounding even gruffer, "so maybe you shouldn't swoon over him."

Deanna stiffened, her mouth dropping open briefly. "I'm not swooning over him!"

"Aren't you?"

"No. I'm happy for them. I think it's really nice. Just so you know, I'm not in the habit of swooning over other women's husbands."

"Good." Mitchell narrowed his eyes at her, and his body felt unusually stiff. "Because you're stuck with me as a husband for three more months."

She wished he hadn't brought up the three more months. She would have been able to indulge in the notion that he was feeling a little jealous, but the reminder of the end date on their marriage made it all rather superficial.

"I know that," she murmured, staring down at her hands in her lap.

After a minute, he wrapped an arm around her shoulders and leaned down to say in her ear, "Sorry. I didn't mean to be grouchy."

She smiled, relieved the tension was over. They normally got along pretty well, and she didn't like when they argued.

When they argued—and when they kissed—things felt out of control.

"I think that's Andrew," she said, going back to their pleasant conversation. She nodded toward a handsome, grinning man chatting to Marietta at the front of the church. "I think he's your kind of guy."

"What do you mean by that?"

"He's one of those charming types who eases through life without many obstacles," she said, making sure her voice was teasing so he wouldn't take it as an insult. "That's what Mandy said, anyway. I've never met him."

"I don't ease through life," Mitchell said. He was frowning in Andrew Damon's direction as if he wasn't liking what he saw.

"Yes, you do," she said in surprise. "You've said so yourself. You don't make things hard on yourself if you can help it. Didn't you say that?"

He was still frowning as his body relaxed. She could feel it, because his arm remained around her. "Yeah. I guess I did." They watched as Andrew threw back his head and laughed, with a kind of good-natured freedom that was impossible to deny. He leaned down to kiss Marietta's cheek before he headed back to the foyer to do his duty as usher.

"I'm not as smarmy as him though," Mitchell said softly, still sounding a little bad-tempered.

"He's not smarmy," Deanna objected. "He looks really nice. He just has that charm thing going on—like you do." When Mitchell wouldn't stop frowning, she asked, "Why do you think it's a putdown? Surely you know that you can talk people around your little finger if you try the least little bit."

"I guess so."

"It's not an insult! I wish I was more like that. I can't charm people into doing anything."

His expression changed as he focused on her again. "Yes, you can."

"No, I really can't. I can make a reasoned argument or I can guilt them into doing something, but I can't charm them with the power of my personality."

"You've got a great personality."

She shook her head, feeling fond and unusually soft even though he wasn't displaying any of his characteristic charm. "Once you get to know me, maybe. But not in general. Did you or did you not think I was boring and vanilla the first time you met me?"

His mouth twisted in amusement. "Well…"

"That's what I thought."

~

Mitchell tried to pay attention to the wedding, but he honestly didn't care all that much about the wedding of people he didn't even know.

The bride was lovely and had the most genuine smile he'd ever seen, and she and Ben Damon seemed to really be in love, but otherwise Mitchell's mind wandered through the ceremony.

He wasn't sure why it bothered him so much that Deanna evidently thought he was shallow and superficial and not inclined to work hard at anything he did.

He'd always admitted to himself he was like that. He'd always assumed it was the only reasonable way to be. But he found himself wishing that Deanna had a better impression of him.

She knew him really well by now—maybe better than anyone except his mother and sister. He hoped there more of him to know than a charming surface.

They went to the reception afterward, and Mitchell smiled and made pleasant small talk with all the people he met. The Damons were big names in the hospitality industry—far bigger than he was. They could be good acquaintances to cultivate. If he was smart, he'd start making inroads now.

But every time he began, he felt Deanna's eyes on him, and he wondered if she thought he was being smarmy.

About an hour into the reception, Deanna hooked her hands in the lapels of his jacket and leaned up to whisper very softly, "What's the matter with you?" Her eyes scanned his face with what looked like concern.

"Nothing." He tried to shake himself out of the strange mood since he didn't want to have to admit it to her. "I'm fine."

"No, you're not. You're acting all weird and… I don't know… repressed or something. Don't you feel like socializing? I thought you'd want to make a lot of contacts here for your business."

"Yeah." He said the one word as a long sigh. "I don't know. I do more than schmooze people with an agenda, you know."

Her eyes widened dramatically. "I know that. I wasn't putting you down. Why did you think I was putting you down?"

He had no good answer for her since he was being ridiculous. "I know you weren't."

"But you're acting like…"

Since he'd somehow managed to hurt her feelings on top of all his other nonsense, he ended up bursting out, "I'm sorry. I don't know what's gotten into me. I just hope you know there's more to me than… than… schmoozing."

She stared at him, clearly baffled by the admission.

Both of them were breathing heavily as they gazed at each other in silence.

Finally she said, "I know there's more to you. *Of course*, I know there's more to you. I didn't at first. I just saw the surface. But I know there's more now. You... you know that, right?"

There was no way he could deny that she was being sincere, and the truth washed over his heart in a way he'd never experienced before. The pleasure was far stronger and far deeper than any lust he'd ever known.

He had no idea what to do with it—this feeling of being understood, appreciated, valued—but he didn't want it to go away.

"Okay," he mumbled since she was obviously waiting for him to say something. "Good."

"Good."

"Good."

Who knew how long they would have extended the silly interaction, but they were interrupted when Cyrus Damon came over to introduce himself since the two men had spoken on the phone a few times in the past.

Cyrus Damon was very important—and making a connection here could really help him. But Mitchell had to struggle to focus on the conversation since his mind kept drifting back to Deanna.

~

They were both quiet on the way back from the church that evening.

Mitchell tried to think of casual conversation, but he was feeling too deep, too intense, too strange to even process, much less push back in order to focus on superficialities.

Deanna seemed to be in a reflective mood as well. She made a few comments about people they'd met but didn't seem inclined to have an extended conversation.

When they got back to the house, they stopped in the entryway and stared at each other.

"Well," Deanna said, gazing up at him, looking a little self-conscious.

"Yeah." Mitchell had no idea what else to say. He wanted to reach out to her, draw her close, somehow show her how he was feeling, but he seemed trapped in a way he didn't understand at all.

"Well," she said again, "Did you want to…" She trailed off, and he didn't know why.

But he did know what he wanted to do. And suddenly he couldn't stop himself.

He reached out for her, taking her head between both of his hands and leaning down into a deep kiss.

She froze just briefly before something seemed to crack inside her, and she was suddenly all in. She grabbed for his neck, arching her soft body into his as she opened to the advance of his tongue.

She moaned in her throat as he claimed her mouth, pouring all his conflicted feeling and tension into the kiss.

When she broke away from the kiss, gasping and still clinging to him, he gathered her up in his arms and carried her toward his bedroom, praying she wasn't going to tell him to stop or pull away.

She didn't seem inclined to do so. After he lowered her onto his bed, she pulled him down on top of her, kissing him eagerly, passionately, as if she'd let all the depth and strength of her true self go at last.

Mitchell was already fully turned on, throbbing with need and a hunger that went far beyond the physical. He was devouring her with kisses, his hands moving over her body, trying to make her feel the same kind of arousal he felt.

She was sweet and passionate and responsive, and everything he felt for her, all of what had been building for the past three months, was pulsing through his body with his blood, with his heartbeat.

He couldn't even speak—it went so deep, it was taking him so strong.

A phone rang in the room, and it took a minute to recognize it was Deanna's.

With a whimper, she pulled it out of her little beaded purse, which was still hooked over her arm, and threw both the phone and the purse off the bed.

Relieved it wasn't a real interruption, Mitchell kissed her again. She was squirming beneath him, and he knew—he knew—she had completely let herself go.

He was reveling in it when the phone rang again from the floor. He growled with annoyance at the second interruption, but she didn't seem inclined to get distracted. Her little hands were reaching for the bulge in his pants, squeezing in a way that made him moan.

He was about to start tearing off clothes when his phone rang. He knew it was his because the ringing came from his pocket.

Surprised and annoyed, he pulled it out, glancing at the screen briefly before he started to throw it on the floor with Deanna's.

But the name on the screen registered and gave him pause.

Panting, he stared at his phone. "It's Kelly. She must be trying to reach you."

Deanna was flushed and gasping, and it obviously took her a minute to process what he'd said. "Kelly? It must be important if she's calling you to reach me."

He nodded and handed her his phone, his erection aching in his pants and somehow knowing it wasn't going to get satisfied after all.

It wasn't.

Deanna's face twisted after she answered and asked Kelly what was the matter.

Something bad had happened. It wasn't going to be their night for sex after all.

NINE

Mitchell eased on the brakes as they approached a stoplight, and he glanced over at Deanna in the passenger seat beside him.

She looked tense and stiff and pale even in the fading light of the evening.

"What exactly did Kelly say?" he asked, his gut roiling in concern after the call she'd received.

Deanna cleared her throat. "She said that Grandmama was in the hospital—and it was serious. She said she fell, but I don't know how a fall could be so—" She broke off as her face twisted. "She was crying. I couldn't really understand her well. She was alone with Grandmama. She must have been so scared."

"Kelly is a smart girl and seems to have a cool head. I'm sure she did fine. And I'm sure your grandmother will be okay. Don't start imagining the worst until you find out exactly what's going on."

He tried to sound encouraging, but he was afraid he just sounded trite and empty. Of course Deanna would be imagining the worst. She'd lived on the edge of everything falling apart for nearly all her life.

He thought about how he would feel if something suddenly happened to Brie or his mother. It would be shock—shock before any of the grief could be processed—since he never expected bad things to happen.

Deanna was different. When he glanced over again, he saw that her hands were twisting restlessly together in her lap, like she was clinging to her hands as the only thing left to hold on to.

He reached over and covered both of her little hands with one of his, not saying anything and not looking from the road as they started to move again.

She didn't speak, but she didn't pull her hands away, so that was something.

He couldn't believe that just fifteen minutes ago, they'd been on the verge of having sex.

He drove as fast as he could to the hospital, getting there in less than twenty minutes. When he got out and walked around the car, he saw that Deanna hadn't moved.

He went to open the passenger door and looked in at her. "Deanna?" he asked softly.

She was still twisting her hands together. "Mitchell, I'm scared." She swallowed visibly. "We laugh at her and get annoyed at her weirdness and complain when she's embarrassing all the time, but we love her. I *love* her."

His heart clenched in sympathy. "I know, baby." He reached in to undo her seatbelt. "But staying in the car isn't going to hold the bad stuff back. Let's go see how she is."

She nodded, her eyes huge and focused up at his face.

When she still didn't move, he stretched his arms out to help her out of the car. Her knees buckled when she stood up, so he kept an arm around her. She leaned on him slightly as they walked into the hospital.

He wondered why it felt strange until he realized that no one ever leaned on him. Not even Brie or his mother. No one truly depended on him for anything.

Until Deanna.

He asked at the front desk and discovered Mrs. Beaufort was in surgery. They were pointed toward a waiting room where they found Kelly, who was sitting alone in a corner, her arms wrapped around herself tightly. She wore her normal two long braids, and they were hanging past her downturned face.

She looked up as they approached, and her face twisted in relief. She jumped up and ran to hug Deanna, who hugged her back for a really long time.

"What happened?" Deanna asked at last, pulling away. She looked a little better now, as if taking care of Kelly had given her stride back. "How did she fall?"

"She fell down the basement stairs."

"What?" Deanna looked horrified. "Why was she—"

"We weren't getting hot water, so we went down to the basement to check. The hot water heater totally died, and it flooded the basement with water. When she saw it, she tried to run down there. She was worried about all her treasures."

They'd moved her collection of historic clothes and knickknacks down to the basement while the house was being worked on—Mitchell knew that much. He could well imagine how the old lady would feel at the possibility of all of it being destroyed.

"Oh, no," Deanna breathed.

"I'm sorry. I should have stopped her. I just—"

"I'm not blaming you. Of course it's not your fault. So how exactly was she hurt? I mean, why is she having surgery?"

"They said she broke a hip and her arm and has a concussion, but at her age, all of it is serious. They seemed really worried about her getting hit on the head like that."

"When did they take her into surgery?" Mitchell asked, putting a bracing hand on Deanna's back. He didn't like the sound of Mrs. Beaufort's injuries at all. He prayed she was going to be okay.

"Just a few minutes ago." Kelly sniffed and wiped her eyes behind her glasses.

"Were you able to reach Rose?"

"Yeah. She's going to fly back right away."

Mitchell remembered that their other sister was in London, where the family she was a nanny for was spending the summer.

When Deanna just stood there, staring at her sister, he gently pushed against her back. "There's nothing to do right now but wait. Why don't you sit down?"

Deanna followed his lead and sat down on the edge of a chair. He moved beside her, trying to think of something he could do to help.

She turned to look at him, appearing almost dazed. "You don't have to—"

"Don't even dare to suggest that I go home," he interrupted gruffly.

Deanna's face contorted briefly with emotion, and Kelly gave him a curious look.

He couldn't figure out the younger girl very well. She was young—just nineteen or so. And she seemed to be blunt and no-nonsense most of the time, but there was something delicate about her too, something sensitive she didn't reveal to the world.

He liked her well enough. A younger sister of his wife could have been a lot more annoying than Kelly. But his thoughts soon turned back to Deanna, who was still kind of perched on her chair like she was ready to jump up at a moment's notice.

"It's going to be a while," he murmured, pulling her back, adjusting her so she was leaning against his side. "You might as well try to relax."

She gave a little snort, but she didn't try to pull away. She breathed deeply and pressed her cheek against his shirt. Mitchell tightened his arm around her, feeling almost comforted by the fact that he might be of some help to her, that she might need him.

He liked that idea, and it was the oddest thing.

No one had ever really needed him before.

He'd never even wanted to be needed before.

~

It was more than two hours later when the doctor finally came out to give them an update.

Deanna had been leaning against him fully, her eyes closed although he knew she wasn't sleeping. Kelly had been curled up on the sofa across from them.

Both of them jumped up when the doctor approached, while Mitchell stood up more slowly. He felt stiff and sore, and his heart started to race as he saw the doctor's face.

"She's stable for now," the doctor said. "But it's serious. We took care of the hip and arm, but there's swelling in her brain, so we'll need to see how long it takes for that swelling to go down and how she is afterward."

"What are the possibilities?" Mitchell asked when Deanna opened her mouth but no sound came out.

"It could be that she's just fine, or there could be some sort of brain damage. We can't tell yet."

"How long will it take for the swelling to go down?"

"It's hard to tell. We should know more tomorrow morning."

"When can we see her?"

"She's in recovery now. We'll move her into a room in an hour or two. There's nothing you can do now, so you might go home and take a shower and get something to eat and then come back later tonight. She likely won't be awake though, so you could just come back tomorrow morning."

Mitchell could tell from Deanna's face that it wasn't going to happen.

When the doctor left, Deanna glanced up at Mitchell. "Do you think you could take Kelly back home?" she asked.

Both he and Kelly started to object at the same time.

"I'm not going home," Kelly said. "I care about her just as much as you do."

"I know. But there's no sense in all of us staying all night. Go on home and get some rest."

"I don't want to go rest while you're here by yourself," Kelly said, sticking out her chin stubbornly. "I'm not a child, you know. You can't just order me around."

Deanna let out a long breath and closed her eyes briefly. "I don't want to order you around. I'm just trying to think of the best thing to do."

"The best thing to do is not for you to sit here all night by yourself," Mitchell put in, strangely pleased when Kelly nodded in support. "Why don't we all go and get something to eat and change clothes, and then when we can figure out the best thing to do."

"I don't want to leave," Deanna said. "I need to be here."

"You don't need to be here. You want to be here because you think you can somehow control things better if you're here. But you can't. There's nothing you can do. So just let go for a few minutes and take care of yourself."

Deanna stared up at him for a minute, as if she were surprised either by the words or the tone, which had been strangely blunt and intimate both.

She didn't nod or agree in words or make any indication that she'd accepted the idea, but she didn't object either, so he put his hand in the middle of her back and pushed her forward.

She walked with him, and the three of them had made it to his car when Deanna finally said, "Wait! I didn't want to leave."

"Tough." He helped her into the passenger seat and then opened the backseat door for Kelly, who hopped in, looking tired but vaguely amused about something.

"What do you all feel like eating?" he asked after he'd gotten into the driver's side.

"I'm not hungry."

"Well, you're going to eat something, so either make a suggestion or put up with whatever we choose."

"A sandwich or something would be good," Kelly said from the back. "Deanna likes the pesto chicken sandwiches at Nick's. It's just down the road here."

"Sounds good. We'll go there."

Deanna shot a look back at her sister, as if she'd betrayed her, but then she turned a glare up to Mitchell, who was clearly the main source of her ire. "You're getting kind of bossy," she mumbled. "What's gotten into you?"

He wasn't sure what had gotten into him—just that he knew he needed to take care of Deanna, and this seemed to be the only way she'd allow him to do it.

He arched his eyebrows with a cool look in response and was rewarded when she gave him a little smile.

~

Deanna's head hurt and her back hurt and her knees hurt and her chest hurt, but she kept trying to mop the pooled water in the basement toward the drain.

She'd stayed at the hospital until lunchtime when Rose had arrived after flying over from London. Since both Rose and Kelly were now at the hospital, Deanna had come over to the house to try to save as many of her grandmother's family treasures as possible.

She'd been working down here for nearly four hours now, and she didn't seem any closer to getting the damage under control.

She'd moved all the boxes to the only dry corner, but she cringed at how wet the bottom of some of the boxes were. A couple had burst open, revealing wet nineteenth-century clothes and curtains.

Her grandmother would be heartbroken if they were ruined.

It didn't seem right that just when things were finally going well for them—the house was being redone and they could show the treasures as they were meant to be shown—this would happen.

It was like the Beauforts were doomed to always get only to the edge of success before the ground fell out beneath their feet.

Deanna straightened up, wincing at the pain in her back, and pulled the elastic out of her hair to redo her ponytail since strands were falling out and sticking uncomfortably to her neck. Once she got some of this water cleaned up, she could start to open the boxes and see how much damage was done. She looked over to where she'd hung up the wet curtains that had survived the Civil War and almost cried at how terrible they looked.

"What the hell are you doing?" roared a familiar male voice from behind her.

She jumped in surprise and nearly dropped her mop. Her back clenched painfully, so she was gasping as she turned around to see Mitchell coming down the basement stairs, dressed in khakis and a green dress shirt. He'd had to go over to the Claremont for a while around noon, and Deanna had hoped he'd be busy all day.

Evidently not.

"I needed to make sure all the family stuff is okay," she said, her voice cracking strangely, like it hadn't been used in too long.

Mitchell was frowning vehemently. He didn't look happy with her at all. "That would have taken about thirty minutes. How long have you been over here?" His eyes ran up and down her body, leaving her feeling naked and exposed. "I thought you were at home resting."

"I'm not tired," she lied, turning her back on him since he was making her feel strangely guilty. "This is important, and the longer these boxes sit in the water, the more damaged they'll get."

He made a growling sound and pulled the mop out of her hands. "I can hire people to do this. You just needed to let me know. You don't have to do it all yourself."

"It's important," she repeated, trying to pull the mop out of his hands, so they ended up having a silly little tug-of-war over it.

He was a lot stronger than her, so he easily won. "It's not that important."

She gasped in outrage, feeling at the end of her emotional rope and so taking everything more personally than she normally would have. "Don't you dare say that! It is important to *us*. This is our family history down here, and it means everything to my grandmother. Just because you don't give a shit about anything doesn't mean you can assume that everyone else is equally heartless."

The annoyance on his face froze for a moment as the words struck home.

She swallowed hard, feeling a wave of guilt and an inexplicable sort of grief. "I'm sorry," she mumbled, turning around and walking over to drag a box away from the water that was slowly edging over to it. "I didn't mean that."

"Yes, you did." He was still standing motionless, looking almost like he'd been struck.

She turned back to the box, on the verge of tears now. "No, I didn't. You can't tell me what I meant or didn't mean. And I didn't meant that."

Her shoulders shook as she tried to hold back tears. She had no idea what was wrong with her. Just that he was Mitchell. He was her husband. And he'd been so sweet lately.

And she'd hurt him when he didn't deserve it.

"Oh, baby, please don't cry."

The rough words only made her cry more, and she ended up leaning over a damp box, strangling on sobs.

He came over to pull her into his arms, and she gasped when the motion made her back catch again.

"What's the matter?" he murmured thickly. "What hurts?"

"Just my back. It's fine."

"No, it's not. You must have been down here for hours. I need to get you home."

"But I told Grandmama I'd save all her treasures." Her grandmother had regained consciousness that morning, and she'd even been able to speak. One of the first things she thought of was all the boxes in the basement.

"I'll get some guys over here right away to take care of it." He was stroking her hair. "Why didn't you ask me earlier?"

"I don't know."

"Yes, you do."

She managed the energy to glare up at him. "Why do you always insist on contradicting me?"

"Because you never tell me the truth."

"I do too."

144

He shook his head slowly. "Not the whole truth. And I want the whole truth from you."

The words disturbed her—deeply. There was no way she could tell him the whole truth, or she'd have to admit that her feelings for him had—quite unwisely—gone far behind the nature of a six-month marriage, no matter how hard she'd tried to keep them under control.

"Well, I wanted to do it myself so I'd have something to do. Something where I felt like I was helping."

"That's what I thought."

She frowned. "If you already knew, then why did you ask?"

"Because I wanted you to tell me."

There was a fond expression in his eyes that was as disturbing as his words, so she pulled away, rubbing her face and then reaching around to rub her back.

"I need to call to see how Grandmama is doing," she said.

"I just called and talked to Kelly. She's been sleeping. She's doing fine. There's nothing you can do right now, so I'm taking you home so you can rest."

"I'd rather—"

"I really don't care what you'd rather do."

She sucked in an indignant breath but didn't have energy to argue. She trudged up the stairs in front of him and then went to his car and climbed in the front seat. As he drove them home, he called up someone to arrange for a crew to get down to the basement to clean it up and save as many of the treasures as possible.

She didn't have the energy to talk, even after he'd hung up, so she closed her eyes and tried to relax. Her head was spinning though, and occasionally she'd jerk with a surge of something akin to panic.

Every time she did, she'd glance over and see that Mitchell was watching her in obvious concern.

It was almost embarrassing, and there was no way to explain the strange behavior, so she just didn't try.

They finally made it home, and he walked around the car to help her out even though she could have managed on her own.

She wasn't used to being taken care of like this. She wasn't used to being taken care of at all.

Everyone had always looked to her to take care of things.

"Are you hungry?" he asked when they were standing in the entryway. It was only yesterday they were standing here in the exact same place and he'd grabbed her into a deep kiss.

She shook her head. "I just want to take a shower."

"Okay."

They walked to her suite, and he went into the bathroom to turn on the shower. When it looked like he was lingering, she pushed him out and closed the door behind him. She took off her clothes and got under the hot water, and for some reason the hot spray caused her to release the building tension, and she sobbed quietly under the shower.

She had no idea what was wrong with her. She was never like this.

She felt a little better though after she'd soaped up, rinsed, and gotten control of herself again. She turned off the water and toweled herself dry, pulling on the tank top and pajama pants she'd been wearing the other night that had been left in the bathroom.

She towel dried her hair as best as possible and then just pulled it into one long braid so it wouldn't get everything wet.

Mitchell was waiting in the bedroom, sitting in a chair, staring worriedly down at the floor.

Her heart was touched at the sight. "I'm fine," she said gently. "I'll just rest some. You can go back to work if you need to or—" She gasped when she moved the wrong way and her back caught again.

It hurt so much she felt the blood drain from her face. She'd thought the shower would help it, but evidently not.

Mitchell's lips tightened as he stood up, but he didn't say anything, which was a relief. She wasn't sure she was able to take another lecture.

He came over to help her walk to the bed, although she would have been okay on her own. "Is it your lower back?" he asked.

"Yeah. I guess I was just bent over for too long. It will be fine once I rest it."

He helped her lower herself onto the bed, and then he turned her over on her stomach. She felt helpless and vulnerable, so she resisted. "Mitchell, I said I'm—"

"You're not fine," he muttered. "So for once, stop being stubborn. I'm not going to hurt you."

Stupidly—so stupidly—she felt on the verge of tears again. "I didn't think you were going to hurt me," she began, feeling like he wasn't understanding her at all. "I just—"

"Shh." He gently adjusted her again so she was on her stomach and started rubbing his hands up and down her back over her clothes. "You don't have to explain."

"But—"

"The longer you distract me by trying to argue, the longer I'm going to stay." His voice was perfectly composed.

The words silenced her since she was feeling so deep and emotional that she thought it best that he get out as soon as possible. Who knew what she would say or do otherwise?"

She let him rub her back gently for a minute, and then he started to focus a massage on her lower back, right where the muscles were catching. It felt incredibly good in a painful sort of way, and she tried to make herself relax instead of resisting.

He didn't speak at all, which was a relief. Just kneaded his strong fingers into her flesh until she couldn't help but groan.

Then his hands moved higher, and he massaged her neck and shoulders until she was moaning even more.

"That's good," she gasped when her body was so relaxed it started responding in an inappropriate way to his touch and the strong presence of him behind her. "Thank you. I feel a lot better."

"Shh." He didn't stop, sliding his hands down to stroke her bottom and thighs.

A tension had tightened between her legs—a familiar pressure that was entirely wrong for the circumstances. He wasn't coming on to her. He was trying to take care of her. She had no idea why her body had quite foolishly misinterpreted the stimulus.

To her relief, his hands finally moved from her bottom and slid up again to her neck until he started to massage her scalp through her hair. That should have been better—less intimate and sensual—but it wasn't.

She was groaning almost helplessly and had to keep her eyes closed in embarrassment, as arousal kept pulsing between her legs.

"Mitchell," she gasped at last. "Please…"

"Please what, baby?" His voice was thick and rough.

"Please stop."

"Why?" He stroked his fingertips down the bare skin of her neck, making her shiver and clench.

"Because I… I…" She was mortified by her reaction, by what he would think of it.

"Aren't you enjoying it?"

"Yes." She gasped far too loud when she felt his hands on her lower back again. Even through her clothes, it felt like sex. "Too… too much."

She felt something shift in his presence, like he'd processed what she meant. Then he was turning her over onto her back so she could no longer hide her face from him.

"Mitchell," she began, her voice cracking and her cheeks hotly flushed.

His face, his eyes, were so tender it took her breath away. She was gazing up at him as his head lowered into a kiss.

She felt boneless, completely exhausted, so she could only respond with her mouth, her lips clinging to his as he brushed them against her so gently.

He was still kissing her—nothing too deep or urgent—when she felt his fingers at her belly, then the waistband of her pants.

She tried to say something but couldn't manage it, too distracted by the kiss.

So she wasn't resisting as his hand slid beneath her underwear to feel between her legs. Her whole body tightened as she felt his finger rubbing her clit, but his touch was so natural, so soothing, that she almost immediately relaxed.

He kept kissing her as he stroked her intimately, bringing her to climax with his fingers and then sustaining the massage until she came again and then again. She couldn't seem to stop it—her body was completely out of her control, like she'd released every piece of her resistance.

Tears were streaming from her eyes as she came yet again, her body tightening briefly with the pleasure but then uncoiling in lingering waves that saturated her completely.

"Enough," she gasped, finally pulling her mouth away from him. "I don't think I can... can take any more."

"Okay." He pressed one more soft kiss on her lips. "Do you feel better?"

"Yes. So good. So good." Each word was a helpless sigh.

"Good."

She was suddenly conscious that his body was desperately tight. He was obviously deeply aroused himself, and he hadn't yet had any release. She reached for his groin almost blindly, so tired she could barely move. "Now we can—"

He moved her hands from his pants. "Not now."

"But—"

"That was for you. You're too tired for anything else." He didn't sound annoyed or frustrated. He still sounded gentle, almost fond.

"But you didn't—"

"I'm not going to fall apart. It wasn't about me. I wanted to do that for you."

He seemed to mean it, and she didn't have the energy to argue anyway. She was so deeply relaxed in almost every way she couldn't keep her eyes open.

"Thank you," she managed to mumble, nestling against his side, under his arm, where it felt warm and safe. "Thank you."

She felt him press a few kisses against her hair just before she fell asleep. "You're welcome, baby."

TEN

Deanna woke up with a tight, deep feeling in her chest—a feeling she immediately recognized as an overly full heart.

She was still in bed, and Mitchell was still beside her. He was sound asleep.

She rolled over on her side so she could see him without turning her head, and she just watched him for a few minutes. He had one arm resting on his belly, and the other was clenched in the covers. His brown hair was a mess—just a little too long—and his eyelashes looked very dark against his skin.

He was still handsome. He was never anything but handsome. But he looked different to her than he usually did. She noticed the wrinkles on his shirt, the way his trousers were hiked up over one calf, the way the hair on his arm looked ruffled rather than lying neatly over his skin.

He felt like a real man—not a handsome stranger, a powerful personality, or a sex god. A human being not all that different than her.

She felt a force of yearning toward him that she'd never experienced before, like she wanted him in every way, like she could see a life with him spreading out before her like a road.

It should have scared her, but the feeling was too consuming to share space in her mind and heart with any other feeling. She reached out toward him, absolutely incapable of resisting the compulsion.

He opened his eyes when she touched his chest, and their eyes met across the short distance between them.

"Hey," he said thickly. "Is it morning?"

"I don't think so." Her hand rested on his shirt, just over his heart. She should have felt silly reaching for him like that, but she didn't. She glanced over at the clock and saw it was just before midnight. With her other hand, she checked her phone and saw that Rose had texted a little while ago, saying their grandmother was doing fine.

She put down the phone, relaxing again.

Mitchell glanced down to where her hand was on his chest, and his expression changed, grew softer. "How are you feeling?" he asked.

She scooted over closer to him, suddenly remembering last night, all last night, all the ways he'd taken care of her. "I feel good."

"Good." He adjusted to wrap an arm around her as she moved closer.

She stretched up to press a kiss against his jaw. "Thank you." Then, feeling far more than she could easily handle, she kissed him again. And again.

He shifted his head so her next kiss landed on his lips, and then he took control of the kiss, cupping the back of her head with one hand and moving his lips against hers hungrily.

He murmured against her mouth, "You don't have to thank me."

"This isn't thanking you," she said, moving over him so her body was pressed fully against his. "This is because I want to."

"Oh, good." Then he kissed her again, sliding his hands down to palm her bottom possessively.

They kissed for a long time, and she reveled in the feel of his big body beneath her, the texture of his skin, the heat that seemed to radiate off him, the hardness of his growing erection. Eventually, they were rocking together in the motion of lovemaking, and she was so turned on she couldn't stay still.

"Mitchell," she gasped, unable to tear her lips away from his.

"Are you ready?"

"Oh, yeah."

He rolled them over, moving on top of her and positioning himself between her legs. Then he started to undress her slowly, kissing all the skin he revealed. He spent a lot of time at her breasts until it was almost torture.

"Okay, Mitchell," she panted, tugging at his hair in an attempt to get him to move on.

He slanted a grin up at her and closed his lips around her nipple, tugging it slightly and making her gasp and arch up.

"Is this some sort of power trip?" she teased. "Because there's never been any doubt that you're able to turn me on."

"Is that right?" He rubbed his jaw against the skin between her breasts, the texture of his bristles making her shiver. "You sure haven't given much evidence of that."

"What is that supposed to mean? You turn me on all the time."

"Really?" He lifted his head, as if he were surprised.

She stared at him, bewildered. "Didn't you know that?"

"I don't know. I do know that I've never had to work so hard at seducing a woman in my life."

She took a minute to process that, and then her cheeks flushed hotly—although she wasn't sure if she was pleased or embarrassed by this knowledge. "That's not because I'm not into you. That's because I'm trying to be smart. And careful."

"Ah." He was smiling as he lowered his mouth again, flicking her nipple with his tongue before he started trailing kisses down her belly. "Well, I'm not going to waste my chance here by taking a shortcut. So try to be patient."

She moaned as desire washed over her, making her squirm her hips as his lips got lower and lower. "I don't want to be patient."

"I don't think patience is required only when we want it to be."

"Jerk."

He shot her a significant look that made her giggle. Then the giggle turned into a whimper as he nuzzled her intimately.

"Mitchell, please," she begged, as he teased her a little longer. She clenched one hand in the covers and tried desperately to hold her hips still. "Oh, please."

He murmured against her arousal as his tongue found her clit, rolling it until she was biting her lip to keep from crying out too loudly as an orgasm tightened inside her.

"Please," she hissed, just before he sucked hard at her clit and she came apart completely, shaking through the spasms of pleasure.

He stroked her gently with his tongue until she'd fully come down. She was gasping out, "Oh God," and "Thank you," as he raised himself over her again and kissed her deeply.

She could taste herself in his mouth, and she didn't even care.

Eagerly, she reached down to unfasten his pants, pushing aside the fabric of his underwear until she was able to free his erection.

She stroked and squeezed him, loving how he jerked and grunted in obvious response.

Then he pulled a condom out of his pocket and rolled it on. His hands were shaking slightly. She noticed it particularly since it seemed a clear sign of how deeply he was affected by their lovemaking.

Just as affected as she was.

With the condom on, he repositioned himself and then guided himself into her slowly. She arched up at the penetration and bent her knees, making room for him in her body.

"You feel so good," he rasped, his mouth just next to hers. "Oh, baby, you feel so good."

"You too." She clutched at his back, wanting to feel him everywhere, wanting to somehow become a part of him and never come out. "It's so incredibly good."

He started to move slowly at first, a leisurely, deep rhythm. She tried to match his motion and not hurry it along, but she felt another orgasm developing that kept urging her on. When she got too eager and jerked her hips, he moved his hand to her bottom to guide her motion, ensuring they were moving together.

For some reason, being so out of control of their speed made the sensations all the more intense. Soon Deanna was stifling cries of pleasure and frustration, and waves of sensation were building slowly at her center.

"Can you come, baby?" he asked, his voice tight with effort. He was working hard to not rush things himself, to make sure it was really good for her, and it meant something to her.

"Yeah." She arched up, fighting again against speeding up their motion, following the guidance of his hand. "Coming. Soon."

The whole world was heating up and blurring, and she could barely take a full breath as the pleasure intensified with each thrust. When it finally broke, she couldn't hold back her cry of release, and it was matched by his as he finally let himself go too.

She could feel him shaking through his climax, saw the pleasure wash over his face, and it filled her with as much satisfaction as her own orgasm.

She held on to him afterward, feeling his body softening against hers.

This was what she wanted. And she didn't want it to end.

Not even three months from now, when their marriage would be over.

She couldn't let herself think about that as he pressed clumsy kisses against her mouth. If she thought about it, then she might come to the inevitable conclusion that she'd just made another big mistake.

~

The next day, Mitchell was in a very good mood.

There were a lot of reasons why he shouldn't be in a good mood. His wife's grandmother was still in serious condition in the hospital. He hadn't gotten much sleep the night before after waking up at midnight. And he had a couple of meetings in the morning that he absolutely couldn't miss.

But he found himself smiling when he was sitting by himself. He felt kind of stupid for feeling that way—it definitely wasn't normal for him—but it simply wouldn't go away.

He was putting stuff up on his desk at around lunchtime, getting ready to head over to the hospital where Deanna had gone first thing when his phone rang.

He picked it up. It was Brie.

"Hey," he said.

"Why didn't you tell me about Deanna's grandmother?" she demanded.

He blinked, completely taken aback by his sister's annoyed tone. "What?"

"Why didn't you tell me about it? It was serious, right? It didn't occur to you to let me know?"

It actually hadn't occurred to him at all. It had never even crossed his mind. "Sorry," he said, feeling a wave a guilt that wasn't characteristic of him either. "I didn't think about it. It just happened—"

"On Saturday. I know. Two days ago. I felt pretty stupid when a friend happened to mention it and I didn't even know. I know it's a weird fake marriage, but you might consider at least pretending it's a normal situation. I mean, poor Deanna. Did you at least try to give her a little support, or have you left her all alone to deal with it while you do your normal thing?"

His guilt transformed to indignation. "I have not left her alone. I'm on my way to the hospital now. Give me a little credit."

"Credit for what? Being sweet and sensitive? Being a loving husband?"

He was about to snap back a reply, but he bit it off as he realized she had every right to question him. He'd never been a sensitive or thoughtful guy. He'd always done what was easiest for him, regardless of other people's needs.

Brie had no reason to assume he'd act any differently with Deanna. In fact, three months ago, he'd told her that was exactly what he intended to do.

When he didn't answer for too long, Brie said, "Shit, I'm sorry. That was going too far. I'm sorry."

Mitchell cleared his throat and shook his head even though there was no way for her to see the gesture. "No, it's fine," he said lightly. "I deserve it."

Now Brie was silent for a minute. Then she said, "What's going on?"

"What do you mean?"

"What's going on? What's gotten into you? You're never like this. You normally blow off any hint of a serious conversation." She paused for a minute and then gasped. "You've fallen for her!"

Mitchell had been in the middle of standing up since he wanted to get to Deanna as soon as possible. But he froze halfway through rising at these words. "Brie, don't be—"

"You've fallen for her!" Brie repeated, a victorious note in her voice. "I knew you'd been acting kind of weird lately, and now it's all making sense. You're crazy about your wife!"

Mitchell was washed with the strangest waves of embarrassment and pride. "Brie, would you st—"

"Don't try to deny it. You're not going to convince me. I seriously wondered if it would ever happen, and now it finally has. Oh, this is fantastic. I can't believe it. I'm so excited!"

"There's nothing to be excited about right now," he said, managing to sound mostly normal.

"Oh, I see." Her tone had changed. "So how are you going to convince her to stay married to you for longer than three more months?"

He had no idea. Absolutely no idea.

But he was sure as hell going to try.

~

Kelly had gone to her college classes today, but both Deanna and Rose were in the hospital room when Mitchell arrived.

He stood in the door and saw that Deanna was sitting in a chair, her head leaning against the wall, looking tired and wan and worried.

His heart went out to her—it actually felt like it was straining in his chest—and he wasn't clueless enough to not recognize the feeling.

He had no idea how or why it had happened, but he loved her. So much he wasn't sure he could contain it.

She glanced over, as if she sensed his presence, and he took comfort in the way her expression transformed on seeing him. Her face relaxed—not into a smile but into a kind of peace and pleasure.

He thought it was a good sign.

She stood up, stepping toward him as he approached. "Mitchell," she said.

He took her hands and reminded himself this was hardly the place for grabbing her into a kiss. "How is she?"

"She's doing better. They say the swelling has mostly gone down. She was awake for quite a while this morning, and they think there isn't any sign of brain damage."

He let out a relieved exhale. "Good. I'm so glad."

Deanna turned her head quickly, as if she suddenly remembered they weren't alone. "This is my other sister, Rose," she said, gesturing toward the pretty and very curvy brunette who was sitting on the opposite side of the hospital bed.

Mitchell stretched his hand out to greet her as she stood up. "It's nice to meet you. I'm sorry we haven't been able to meet before."

"I know," Rose said, smiling and looking a little curiously from her sister to Mitchell. "I was in London all summer with my family."

"Her family" must be how she referred to the family she was a nanny for.

She added, "But I've heard a lot about you."

"I bet you have. Hopefully, you didn't hear anything too bad."

"Oh, it wasn't…" Rose stuttered to a stop, looking a little self-conscious. "Well, I did hear about the Pride."

Mitchell groaned, remembering how ridiculous he must have looked in his shock over seeing the dead cats in the midst of his sneezing attack. "Great."

Deanna gave a little laugh. "He's had a lot of good moments to make up for that."

Smiling down at her, he had to resist the impulse to cup her face. He'd moved closer without being conscious of doing so.

When Deanna pulled away from him again, he saw that Rose was giving them more curious looks.

Then she said, "I got some lunch earlier, but Deanna hasn't had any. Maybe you could take her to get something to eat?"

"I'm fine—" Deanna began.

"That's a good idea," Mitchell said, at the same time, talking over her and pairing the words with a hand on her back. "We won't be too long."

Deanna slanted him an annoyed look as they walked out. "You're going to have to get over the habit of bossing me around or your balls aren't going to make it for three more months."

Mitchell chuckled, although he didn't like her reference to the three months, as if she never questioned the fact that their relationship would be over for sure at the end of the contracted time.

"I'll work on it," he murmured as they entered the elevator.

"I don't believe you."

"What don't you believe?"

"I don't believe you'll work on it." She was smiling and looked fond, but his heart took a sudden nosedive as she said, "You like being bossy, and you don't work on anything, if you can help it, so I don't think you'll be working on not being bossy."

She was teasing, he knew, but she meant it. It would never cross her mind that for the first time in his life he might want to work on something—even if it was hard.

~

That evening, Mitchell was heading back up the elevator, going to pick up Deanna and take her home.

Her grandmother was recovering, and there didn't seem to be any permanent damage. She was still really weak with the broken bones and the head injury, so she'd have to stay in the hospital for several more days.

But things were definitely looking up.

He got off the elevator and started in the direction of her room when he saw a small dark-haired figure standing in front of the windows in a sitting area across from the elevator. Her back was toward him, but there was no way he wouldn't recognize the long thick hair, the shapely ass, the graceful curve of her neck.

He walked over toward his wife, wrapping his arms around her from behind when he reached her.

She jerked slightly, as if surprised, but then relaxed back against him. "She told me to leave," Deanna explained. "The physical therapist had come in, and she didn't want me there. She doesn't like anyone to see her when she's weak."

"Hmm," Mitchell murmured, pressing a few kisses against her hair. "That sounds familiar."

"I'm not that bad."

He actually laughed since she seemed to sincerely believe this was true.

"I'm not," she said, sounding slightly confused. "I'm just..." She trailed off, as if she was thinking about the words.

"You're just what?" he asked, curious about what she was going to say.

She sighed. "I don't know." She eased forward, trying to pull out of his arms, but he wouldn't let her. "Mitchell," she began. "I'm not sure..."

"Have you been standing here trying to talk yourself into being smart and reasonable?" he asked, his voice a low murmur as he turned her around in his arms and leaned down to kiss her softly.

"Maybe a little," she admitted, her arms going up around his neck.

He loved how she couldn't seem to help reaching out for him, as if her body responded to his almost against her will.

"Well, I think the smart, reasonable thing would be to go get some dinner and then go home and have sex."

She shook with suppressed laughter, even as she let him kiss her again. "So that's the most reasonable thing, is it?"

"Absolutely. It's just what the doctor ordered. I'm nothing if not a reasonable guy."

She was smiling and relaxed, and he was already getting excited about what might happen that evening. He wanted to go even further. He wanted to tell her what he was feeling. But he realized now that it would be a mistake.

She was still thinking only of a six-month marriage, and she wasn't even sure about committing to that with him. If he suddenly burst out that he was crazy in love with her and wanted to spend the rest of his life with her, she would be dumbfounded, utterly shocked.

And the worst part was, she wouldn't believe him.

ELEVEN

A few hours later, Deanna was tangled up in Mitchell's body, both of them hot and panting and a little sweaty.

She was feeling relaxed and really good after an incredible round of sex, but she was also feeling dangerously close to him—close to him in a way that she knew was utterly stupid.

He was into her. There was no way she could doubt that. But he was the kind of guy who threw himself into whatever he was doing at the moment—and then he'd move on without a second thought once it was over.

He'd told her he wanted to make the best of their marriage, and that was what he was doing.

But she was different. She couldn't move on so easily. And she was sure—even now—she would be crushed when this was over, and if she let herself get even deeper with him, she might never get over it.

She'd never really been in love before—not completely, anyway. She'd always held a little of herself back, even in the two relationships she'd had that she thought had potential.

There was no potential here, and she was having to fight to hold any of herself back.

She'd needed him, so she'd let things go further than they should have, but now was the time she had to be strong.

Mitchell's body had softened beneath her, and his hand was gently stroking her hair. It seemed pretty clear he wasn't intending for them to move anytime soon.

She wanted so much to stay, to nestle against him like she had the night before, but that would be weak, would be foolish, would be everything she'd made sure she wasn't all her life.

People depended on her. Her grandmother and Kelly and Rose. She couldn't let herself fall apart.

So with great force of will, she rolled off him, their damp skin clinging where it had been pressed together.

"Where are you going?" he muttered, trying to pull her back against him.

"I'm tired," she said lightly. "I'm going to bed."

"That sounds good to me." His hair was mussed from the way she'd been tugging at it in her passion before, and his expression was almost sweet. "So stay here in bed with me."

"I'm going to sleep in my room." She managed to roll off the bed and stand up, although she was a little sore and she felt chilled in the room away from the heat of his body.

"Why?" His brows had drawn together, and he definitely didn't look pleased.

If she gave him a real reason, or any kind of excuse, he would argue, so she said instead, "Because I want to. Is there a problem with that?"

He stared at her for a long time, emotion she couldn't recognize reflecting on his face. "I guess not. I just don't understand why you want to."

She felt guilty because he was disappointed, but that was ridiculous. "You don't have to understand. You just have to respect my choices. That's how things are supposed to work between us."

"I know. But it seems like maybe you want to stay with me, and I don't like that you're making yourself do something against your own wishes."

He was being serious—far more serious than he normally was—so she didn't want to blow him off, although that was her first instinct, just to get away as fast as she could. "It's not against my wishes. I see what you're saying, but I think you're reading me wrong."

He was silent for a moment, and she had no idea what he was thinking. "Okay. I'll see you in the morning."

Relieved and upset and ludicrously let down, she grabbed her clothes and headed back into her own suite.

Her rooms were just as lovely and comfortable as they'd always been, but they felt lonely tonight.

~

The next day, Mitchell and Deanna had scheduled to have dinner with George and Gina Fenton.

The restaurant deal was moving quickly, and the lawyers had drawn up the contract, so there were just a few more details to work out before the sale was officially closed.

Deanna should have been happy about it since it meant the main purpose of the marriage was complete. But the thought of it just made her feel a little sick.

Once the deal was done, she wondered if she should suggest ending their marriage early so things wouldn't get any more complicated than they already were.

It seemed like that was probably the wisest decision to make. She just didn't want to make it.

She'd done her duty to her family. The work on the house was more than halfway complete. She could pull back now without any betrayal, and then maybe she could start down the very difficult road of getting over Mitchell.

If her feelings got any deeper, she was afraid she'd never get over him.

Mitchell sure wasn't making it easy on her though.

All evening he'd been acting like Prince Charming, acting sweet and seductive and funny and romantic. His act must have been convincing to the Fentons. Honestly, it was almost convincing Deanna.

"You look gorgeous tonight," he murmured into her ear, as they waited at the entrance of the restaurant for the valet to bring up their car after dinner was over. "Have I told you that?"

"Several times," she said, trying to sound light and good-humored although her heart, body, and mind were an uproar of need and longing and confusion and fear. "But George and Gina are too far away to hear us, so you don't need to keep laying it on so thick."

"I wasn't," he said, stiffening slightly. She could feel it quite clearly since his body was pressed up behind her, one of his arms wrapped around her. "I meant it. You look absolutely beautiful."

She sighed, fighting the instinct to pull away from him. "Thank you." She wore a dark green dress that made her eyes look greener than they were, and she'd pulled her hair up in a French twist. She felt unusually elegant and sophisticated.

And strange. Like it wasn't quite her.

Mitchell tilted his head and ran a line of featherlight kisses against her cheekbone and down toward her jaw. "You have no idea how much I love the curve of your neck right here." He brushed the side of his index finger along her throat, making her shiver again. "It drives me crazy."

She wanted to lean into his words, have them surround her like a blanket. But she knew they didn't mean what she wanted them to mean. "It's just a normal neck."

"It is not a normal neck. There's nothing normal about it." He leaned farther down to press a soft kiss against her throat. "There's nothing normal about you."

It sounded like he meant it, and there was no reason to assume he didn't. At the moment, he was into her, and it was nice. It made her feel good. *Really* good.

It just wasn't enough.

She leaned her head away, trying to discreetly pull away from his kisses.

He noticed the gesture immediately and straightened up. "What's wrong?"

"Nothing." Her throat was tight with emotion, but she tried to speak naturally over the lump. "I just think the Fentons are fully convinced we're a normal couple, so you can back off a little on the romantic act."

He turned her around to face him and took her face in both of his hands, cupping it gently. "I don't think you want me to back off. I think you *like* the romantic act."

God help her, she did. But she wanted it to be more than an act.

He kissed her on the mouth, and she responded for a few seconds before she made herself pull away.

He let out a frustrated exhale. "What is the matter, Deanna? You can't tell me you don't want this. I know you do. So why don't you just let go and enjoy the moment?"

There. He'd made it clear again. This was just about the moment for him, and it was about a lifetime for her.

"Of course I like to kiss you," she said, feeling a sudden surge of desperation and trying frantically not to fall apart and make a huge fool of herself. "Of course I'm attracted to you. But what my body wants isn't necessarily what *I* want. Don't you understand that?"

He stared down at her, something almost frozen in his expression.

"You can seduce me if you want, and I may end up relenting and falling into bed with you, but that's not going to change anything that matters." She cleared her throat when her voice wobbled. "There are things that are important to me, Mitchell. The most important things in the world to me. I really like you, and I think you're a great guy, and I'm insanely attracted to you. But sex with you and a six-month marriage of convenience just aren't the most important things in my world."

He still looked frozen, and she was momentarily afraid she'd genuinely hurt his feelings.

"It's nothing personal," she added quickly, reaching up to put a hand on the lapel of his jacket. "I really do think you're great, and not just because you're so hot. But I don't know how to say this more clearly. I hope… I hope… you'll respect my wishes."

"Of course." He took a step back, dropping his arms and clearing his throat the way she had the minute before. "Of course I will. I didn't mean to… If this isn't what you want, then I won't press it on you."

His words didn't sound quite right. He made it sound like there was something about him—who he was—that she didn't want.

And she did want him. She wanted all of him.

She just didn't want what he was willing to offer her.

~

That evening, after Deanna went to her suite for the night, Mitchell went outside for a run. He usually worked out on the equipment he had in the house, but he felt like running tonight and the house was claustrophobic.

It was almost midnight when he set off, and he ran in the dark, forcing himself to keep going even after the fatigue set in and sweat was dripping down into his eyes.

He wondered if he could keep running whether eventually his heart would stop hurting so much. Maybe if his body hurt deeply enough, he wouldn't feel the far deeper pain.

Deanna didn't want him. All of what he'd been sensing in her—the attraction, the need, the hunger, the comfort—was mostly physical, and she didn't want him in any other way.

Even when he made a point of not putting any pressure on her—making sure she knew he didn't want any more than the moment—she still didn't want him enough.

It made sense. He'd always stood for everything she wasn't, and all of what she held most dear he'd spent his life brushing away.

There was no reason she would want to spend her life with someone like him. He'd never proven to her—to anyone—that he could commit to a relationship so permanently.

She'd been utterly serious when she spoke to him at the restaurant. She wasn't going to change her mind.

He'd taken his phone, and when he heard it vibrate with a new text, he slowed down and pulled it out to check, vaguely hoping it was Deanna.

It wasn't. It was Brie.

Do you and Deanna want to come over for dinner tomorrow?

Even the casual question hurt Mitchell since it seemed to represent everything he couldn't have. Wiping the sweat off his hands and face with his shirt, he texted back. *I can come. Not sure about Deanna.*

He thought the reply sounded light and impersonal enough, but evidently Brie sensed something wasn't right.

His phone rang, and when he picked up, Brie demanded, "What's wrong?"

"What do you mean?"

"What's wrong between you and Deanna?"

He was still walking, still breathing fast and shallow. "Nothing. It was just a normal reply."

"No, it wasn't. Has something happened? I thought you were going to convince her to stay married to you."

He let out a sigh that was too long and too loud. "She doesn't want to be convinced."

Brie paused for a moment. "I don't think that's right. I saw her with you at the hospital yesterday night. I think she's into you too."

"Not in that way. She doesn't want me."

For some reason, the words sounded final, tragic, heartbreaking. His throat hurt so much he couldn't breathe.

"Shit, I'm sorry. Did you... did you ask her?"

"In a way. She made it clear."

"Well, you can't just ask her in a way. Ask her for real. Maybe she doesn't know you're serious. She's the kind of girl who's only going to let herself fall in love with a man when there's a real future. She's not a temporary or casual kind of girl. You know that. And you're like the epitome of the temporary, casual guy. Maybe she doesn't know you've changed, that you want something different."

He felt a ridiculous spark of hope. Maybe that was true. Maybe she really didn't know—even though he thought his feelings should have been obvious to anyone with a pair of eyes. "She's all about playing it safe and making good decisions," he said slowly.

"See? I bet that's all it is. She thinks you're not safe because you've always before just done whatever was easy. You need to prove to her that you can be in it for the long haul. That you can do the hard thing when you want it badly enough."

He did want Deanna that much. He wanted her so badly he couldn't take a full breath.

"Okay," he said, almost swallowing over the one word. "Okay."

His heart was soaring now, the way it had been sinking earlier. It made sense. It was exactly right for who Deanna was and who he'd always been himself.

"Go talk to her," Brie said, sounding as excited as he felt. "Go talk to her right now."

"Okay."

"And call me back as soon as you can!"

After he hung up, he stared at the phone for a minute, and then he put it back in his pocket and started to run.

He was two miles from his house, but he sprinted all the way, finally arriving soaked with even more sweat and so breathless he could barely see.

He went immediately to her suite and pounded on the door.

After a moment, he pounded again and called out, "Deanna? Are you asleep?"

She swung the door open, staring at him in bewilderment. "Well, if I was asleep before, I sure wouldn't be now. What the hell is going on? Are you okay?" Her eyes scanned his face and body with what looked like concern.

Her concern made his heart tighten with sentiment, but he was here now, so he burst out, "I wanted to talk. To you. About our marriage."

Her face changed. She dropped her head to look at the floor so quickly he couldn't read her expression. "Oh. Actually, I was thinking about that too."

"You were?" He was still gasping and breathless, and he could barely see through the sweat.

"Yeah. I was just lying in bed thinking about it and trying to figure out what to do. Things have gotten… I don't know… weird and complicated between us."

It was true. He stared at her, wondering blindly if she'd come to the same conclusion he had.

"And I think we should probably do something about it. This weird limbo isn't good for either of us." She sucked in a shaky breath.

Mitchell stood, motionless and speechless, his heart beating in his chest, his head, his ears.

"So," Deanna said, her voice breaking. "So… I was thinking. Once the restaurant deal goes through, maybe we should just end the marriage early. Before the six months are over, I mean."

~

Deanna wasn't sure what to expect from Mitchell after she'd burst out with the conclusion she'd come to after brooding and crying over the situation for too long.

She thought maybe he would go along with it just to make things easier—or else maybe have some real objections, which she would have been willing to listen to and discuss.

She certainly wasn't expecting what happened.

"No."

She blinked in surprise at the blunt response. She couldn't read any expression on his face. He just looked blank.

Since he was clearly out of breath from running and was still gasping heavily, she paused, waiting for him to continue—maybe after he'd caught his breath and processed what she'd said.

But he just kept standing there, his gray eyes far darker than normal and his hair wet with perspiration. "No," he said again.

"No?" She rubbed her face, trying to make herself think clearly. This whole thing had become such a mess there probably wasn't any way out. "What do you mean, no?"

"I mean no. We're not going to end the marriage early. It hasn't been six months."

If he'd looked hurt or upset or even angry, she might have been hopeful that he was feeling something just a little similar to her. But he wasn't any of those things. He was almost hard—and he grew harder as the moments passed.

"I know it hasn't," she said, trying to be reasonable. "And if it really helps your business stuff to stay married for the final three months, then of course I'll do it. But all you wanted out of this marriage was the restaurant deal, and once it goes through I don't understand why you'd object."

"It doesn't matter whether you understand or not. You shouldn't be trying to renege on our deal."

"I'm not trying to renege." Her voice cracked because she was getting really upset now. She didn't understand why he was acting this way. "I'm not. I was just offering another possibility—one I thought would work well for both of us."

"Why would it work well for *me*?"

"Because you could move on with your life. Isn't that what you want?" Her voice trembled slightly on the last question. Everything was so strange and confused and not at all like it should be.

Mitchell wasn't acting at all like he would normally act.

"My life is fine right now. I thought yours was too. If there's something about our marriage that isn't working for you, just tell me what it is, and we can make adjustments if necessary."

Her eyes widened at his impersonal tone. She couldn't believe this was the man she'd just made love to the previous day. "I already told you. I don't think it's a good idea to get intimate like… like we were. I told you that from the beginning, but you keep…" She trailed off since it was hardly his fault they'd had sex the times they had. Both of them were responsible for what had happened.

"I won't come on to you again. Is there something else you're not happy with?"

"I don't understand. Are you saying you want to stay married to me? Are you… are you happy with the way things are?"

"I think I've made it clear that I am."

He had. In some ways, he'd been like a different person recently—at least a person she'd never seen in him before. "I think we need to be careful though," she said. "You've been so sweet to me this week. I really appreciate how you've been there for me. But I don't think we can assume it means more than it does. It's just because you're a nice guy and I've been really needy. Despite how you act sometimes, you really have a good heart. It's not necessarily—"

He made a strange rough sound in his throat. "What the hell are you talking about? You've got me totally wrong. I'm not a nice guy. I don't have a good heart. And not once in my life have I ever been sweet. None of that has any bearing on this conversation right now."

She hugged her arms to her chest, hating the sound of his clipped tone. He wasn't like this. Not really. Not at heart. She had no idea why he was acting like this now.

Unless she'd hurt his feelings somehow.

He'd told her that he got mean when he felt rejected.

She hated the thought of it, and scrambled to fix whatever she might have done. "I'm really sorry. I wasn't trying to hurt you or act like I don't appreciate everything you've done. You know I really like you. I think you're great. And obviously—"

"You've already told me all this."

"But I don't want you to think I think there's anything wrong with you."

"You just don't want to be married to me any longer than you have to."

The way he said it sounded horrible—sounded like the worst kind of insult she could have given him—when that was the last thing in the world she would have wanted. "I'm so sorry," she said, feeling her eyes start to burn as the emotion became too powerful. "I didn't mean any of it to come across like this. I don't know what to say."

"I think you've already said it." His eyes were focused on her, but she wasn't sure they were even seeing her even more. "You like me. You think I'm great. But you're ready for this marriage to be over—because I'm not the person you really want."

"That's not..." She choked since all this was so incredibly wrong.

When she couldn't continue, he asked, "That's not what you meant?" For just a moment, he sounded almost human again.

She was trying so hard to be honest—as honest as she possibly could—but everything she said seemed to be wrong. "It's not that I don't want you—in a lot of ways. It's just that we're so different. We want and believe in entirely different things. We're looking for different things out of life. So you can't... you can't be the person... the person..."

"The person you really want."

She nodded, tears streaming from her eyes. Because it was true. It was absolutely true. And not admitting it wouldn't be fair to either one of them.

She wanted Mitchell. She loved him. She wished she could spend her life with him. But he would never be a man who could give that to her.

He didn't believe in marriage. He didn't have any interest in starting a family. He brushed aside history and tradition and ceremony like they were meaningless trivialities.

Even if he might want to be with her now, they could never be happy together because they would always, forever want different things.

Mitchell wanted what was easy, what felt good at any given moment.

And Deanna had always only wanted what would truly last.

"Do you understand now?" She gasped, trying to control her tears. "Don't you think it's better to just end the marriage as soon as possible so we don't end up hurting each other even more? I really think that's the wisest thing."

"I don't care what you think is wise," Mitchell said curtly. "Our contract says we stay married for a full six months, and I'm going to hold you to that."

She gasped again, this time in sharp pain, like someone had slashed her with a knife.

When her eyes cleared, she saw that his expression was hard, merciless.

Maybe he was hurt, maybe he felt rejected, but the man she really wanted would never use marriage vows like a weapon—any more than he'd spontaneously come up with the idea of marriage as an easy way of making a business deal.

He didn't see marriage the way she did, and he clearly never would.

There was no way she could speak through the grief and pain that was overwhelming her, so she just nodded—to show she understood what he said and wasn't going to object—and then took a step back and closed her bedroom door on his face.

Just over two months now. She could make it through.

Her heart had already been broken, so at least there wasn't anything left to break.

TWELVE

Mitchell stood in front of Deanna's closed door and heard her crying on the other side.

She was trying to stifle it—that much was obvious—but she wasn't successful.

It was brutal—the twisting of his heart, over and over again. First because she wanted to end the marriage. Then because she was so open and blunt about not wanting the man he really was. And now because he'd obviously hurt her in his natural instinct to be mean as a way of holding himself together and protecting the last shreds of his heart.

He could stand the battering of his own self, but he simply couldn't stand for it to happen to Deanna. So instead of turning around and going to his room to take a shower and pull himself together, he pounded on the door again.

"Mitchell, please just go away!" she wailed, choking on more sobs.

He swung the door open and saw that she'd collapsed in a heap on her bed. He strode over, pulling her up and into his arms. She kept sobbing against him, even though he was soaked with sweat and had just treated her so cruelly.

"I'm sorry," he murmured. "Deanna, please don't cry. I'm sorry."

"I'm… sorry too." She clung to him, and he held her as tightly as he could, as if all the aching need in his soul was channeled into this one grip. "I'm so sorry, Mitchell. I didn't mean to hurt you."

"I hurt you too. I never wanted to do that."

She cried for a little longer, but then she finally started to calm down. That meant he should release his hold on her, but he simply didn't want to.

This might be the only way he was allowed to touch Deanna now, and he didn't want it to end.

She sniffed and cleared her throat and finally pulled away. He had no choice but to release her.

"You're all sweaty," she said with a teasing little smile that unclenched his heart.

"I just ran about seven miles."

"It's stupid to run that far in the middle of the night."

"I sometimes do stupid things."

"So do I."

They gave each other sheepish looks until Deanna's expression relaxed into a full smile. "We've made a real mess of this whole thing."

He sighed. "I know. I don't know what to do about it."

"Well..." She took a deep breath, obviously thinking hard. "Well, we've got two more months, so maybe we should just try to be... be friends. I don't want to lose you, Mitchell, and I don't want to hurt you again."

"Me either," he admitted, although his chest was still twisting because she obviously didn't want from him what he wanted from her.

But still... this would be better than nothing. And there was no reason to assume her feelings for him would never change.

They had attraction and understanding and shared humor and camaraderie.

Maybe, if she grew to trust him, they could have love too.

He wanted it now. All of it—all of her—right now. He felt like he'd been waiting forever for her, and he didn't want to wait anymore.

But Brie was right. Deanna cared about him a lot, yet she believed he would never do the hard thing.

She was wrong though. Maybe he'd been like that before, but that was because there hadn't been anything he wanted enough to work for.

He wanted Deanna that much. He would do anything he needed to do—work as hard as he had to work, wait as long as he had to wait—in order to get her at last.

"Mitchell?" Deanna asked softly, after he was silent for too long. "Is that… is that all right?"

He nodded, reaching over and putting a hand over hers, resisting the urge to touch her any more than that. "Yes. It's all right."

~

"So you're not going back to London?" Deanna asked her sister, as they were sitting in her grandmother's parlor a couple of weeks later.

"No." Rose's flashed a little dimple over her sip of iced tea, a sure sign that she was feeling self-conscious about something. "Jill, Julie, and Mr. Harwood are coming back to Savannah next week anyway, so he said there wasn't any need for me to fly all the way back. He said he could manage."

Kelly had been puttering with an old mantle clock which hadn't worked in years. She was determined to one day get it fixed and kept returning to work on the mechanism when she had nothing else to do. "How long have you been working for the Harwoods, Rose?"

Rose looked surprised. "For two years. You know that."

"And he still expects you to call him Mr. Harwood?"

"He's never said anything, but it would hardly be appropriate for me to go around calling him James. He's my employer. Not my friend."

"Still, I'd think you'd have gotten to know each other well enough. What does he call you?"

"Rose." She stared down at her glass. "Rosie, actually."

Deanna almost choked on her sip. "Rosie? No one calls you Rosie. How does he get away with that?"

With a slight flush of her cheeks, Rose admitted, "Well, honestly, I think he just got my name wrong initially, and then he'd called me Rosie for so long he couldn't change it to my real name."

"Maybe you don't want him to change it," Kelly teased, giving her sister a wry look over her glasses.

Rose narrowed her eyes. "Don't be ridiculous. He's my boss. Besides, he's engaged anyway."

"What?" Deanna straightened up. James Harwood's wife had died two and a half years ago, shortly before he hired Rose. "He's engaged? When did this happen?"

"A few weeks ago. But the wedding is not until next year."

"Is he still going to want a nanny for Jill and Julie after he gets married?"

Rose gave a little shrug. "He said he would. I guess it depends on what his fiancée thinks, but I've met her and I don't really think…" She cleared her throat delicately. "She's not exactly the maternal kind. I think she'll want to keep a nanny, if only so she doesn't have to bother with the girls."

They were all silent as they took in this piece of information. Deanna had met Rose's employer a few times, and he seemed like a decent guy—kind of absent-minded and sometimes grumpy. She thought he could probably do better than marrying a woman who wasn't excited about having two stepdaughters. That might make it difficult for Rose.

Their grandmother had been napping in her chair, which she often did in the afternoons after her injury. But she must not have really been asleep because she opened one eye and said, "He will make an appropriate husband."

The three sisters looked at each other a little warily, but none of them asked for further explanation. Maybe she meant he'd make an appropriate husband for his fiancée, but Deanna rather doubted it. She started to worry for Rose.

"Speaking of husbands," her grandmother continued, "I haven't seen yours lately, Deanna. Where is he?"

"Right now? I guess he's at work. Where else would he be?"

"Why has he not paid me a visit since I've gotten out of the hospital?"

"He's been busy, but I'm sure he will if you'd like him to. He can't come over here though. He's allergic to the Pride."

"I would like to thank him for saving our treasures." Her grandmother glanced over to the rack of old dresses, which had been carefully washed and repaired and were in even better condition than they'd been before.

"I'll tell him you said thanks."

"What's going on with him, anyway?" Rose asked.

Deanna swallowed. She'd managed to avoid any talk about Mitchell for the past couple of weeks, but it was inevitable eventually. "What do you mean? He's fine."

"I mean, what's going on between you? At the hospital, it looked like you were... more than a business arrangement. But now you're hanging out here half the time."

With a shrug, Deanna said, "We get along pretty well. But it's just a six-month thing, you know."

"Why?" That was Kelly, who was leaning forward now, the clock momentarily forgotten. "He's crazy about you. Anyone can see."

"No, he isn't. He likes me well enough, but he's not the kind of guy who's in it for the long haul. You know what he's like as much as I do."

"Maybe he can change. It does happen sometimes, you know."

Deanna shook her head. "We've gotten it worked out. When the six months are over, we'll get the divorce—just like we always planned."

It still hurt to say it out loud, but she kept telling herself the truth over and over again so she wouldn't forget it. She and Mitchell had been getting along pretty well for the past couple of weeks since the blowup that night. They had dinner together fairly often. They sometimes had breakfast together, and sometimes they worked out together, and sometimes they hung out to watch TV. It wasn't exactly the same as it had been before—both of them were too careful about keeping an appropriate distance. But it was certainly better than the brewing angst and tension that would invariably explode into pain.

They were both mature adults. They could work out a reasonable agreement without either of them falling apart.

It was the best Deanna could hope for in this situation.

"That was always the plan," her grandmother said in a somber voice, which was vaguely disturbing since her eyes had closed again.

All three of them jumped slightly.

"What do you mean?" Deanna asked, feeling a shiver of anxiety slice down her spine.

"That was the plan. End the marriage at six months. Then, after the divorce, you can make yourself available to Morris Alfred Theobald III. He was very disappointed when you got married."

Deanna's stomach churned. "What? I'm not going to make myself available to that man. I don't even like him."

"You will learn to like him," her grandmother said, her eyes still closed. "He will make a good husband. You will get divorced, and we will have him over for dinner."

She said the words as if they were the pronouncement of fate, as if they were truth from on high.

Kelly and Rose were silent and tense, and Deanna's spine was very straight as she heard herself saying, "No. I'm not going to have dinner with him. I'm never going to marry him or even date him. I don't want Morris Alfred Theobald III. I'm not even sure I want to get divorced at all."

She couldn't believe she was saying no to her grandmother like this. She'd never done anything like it in the past. Rose and Kelly were clearly shocked, but Rose got over it first.

She leaned forward and asked, "Really, Deanna? I'm so happy to hear that because I think you two are really good together. I think you should keep him."

"I think you should keep him too," Kelly added.

Deanna's mind was still reeling from what she'd just said, and she almost choked on hearing her sisters' words. "I can't keep him! I don't know what I was even talking about just now. The six months is in the contract and everything. Plus we're totally different. He doesn't believe in marriage. He only commits to temporary relationships. He thinks all our treasures are clutter, and he thinks the Pride is creepy!"

"The Pride is a little creepy," Kelly whispered, eyeing their grandmother, who still had her eyes closed and a frown on her face.

"He said he doesn't believe in marriage because he'd never been there himself," Rose said. "I really think it's just because he'd never known what he was missing. And he wasn't really being honest when he said he only knows how to commit to temporary relationships. He's committed to his mother, isn't he? Look at the lengths he's gone to make her happy. That is commitment. He can commit."

Deanna stared at Rose and then at Kelly and then her grandmother.

"Think about it," Rose added.

"That's what I was trying to say all along," Kelly said. "Not that he's changed, necessarily. Just that he wasn't who everyone always thought he was. Even who *he* thought he was."

"But…" Deanna couldn't finish as she thought through what had been said and whether or not it could be true.

He'd agreed to ending their marriage, and he wasn't acting like he was really into her the way he had before, so it was hard to know whether to feel hopeful or not.

But maybe—just maybe—she was allowed to feel a little hope. Not all the way. She really didn't want to be any more foolish than she'd already been, but still…

Perhaps a marriage of more than six months wasn't quite as impossible as she'd always assumed.

She glanced back at her grandmother and blinked in surprise.

The old woman's eyes were still closed, but on her face was the slightest hint of a smile.

~

Mitchell glanced at the clock. It was almost ten o'clock, and Deanna still wasn't home.

She'd gone out to eat with her sisters since Rose's employer was getting back in town the following day so Rose would have to go back to work.

Deanna had said he could come along if he wanted, but he'd refused since it felt like he'd be intruding on sister time and he was trying very hard not to be too pushy or intrusive with her.

Now he was regretting his restraint. He hadn't seen Deanna all day since he'd had an early meeting and had been gone before she got up.

He saw her little enough as it was now—sometimes just an hour or two a day—and he couldn't help but begrudge anything that stole the time he might otherwise have with her.

Instead of stewing on his complaints, he tried to focus on his task. It was detail work, and his hands were big and not particularly delicate.

He looked down at the beads and suddenly felt like an idiot. What the hell was he doing, anyway? He wasn't doing a very good job. Deanna would probably have to completely redo it. She would laugh at him for thinking this was an appropriate project for him to tackle.

But he had gotten it in his head a few weeks ago, after they'd agreed to try to be friends, and now that he'd started, he wasn't going to stop.

It was taking forever though. He didn't know how Deanna had patience to work with these tiny beads all the time. He'd been working tonight for an hour on it, and his fingertips were almost numb and his eyes were glazing over. He pressed on, however.

It was going to take a really long time to get this done, and he only had just over a month left to go.

When he heard a car approaching the house, he put the work down and then tucked the supplies in a big drawer so Deanna wouldn't happen to see it. She was never in his room now anyway, but still... she definitely couldn't see this until he was finished.

Shaking himself off, he walked downstairs just as Deanna was coming in through the front door.

She smiled at him. "Hey, you."

"Hi." His instinct was to reach out for her since she looked so pretty and flushed and feminine and *his*. But he resisted the urge and instead asked, "How was dinner?"

"It was good," she said, dropping her purse on the floor and staring down at it. "It was really, really good."

He chuckled. "Did you maybe have a couple of drinks?"

"Just a few."

Laughing, he picked up her purse from the floor and put it on the table where she always kept it. "Good. You should have a good time more often."

"I did have a good time." She was smiling at him, almost tenderly, and she reached out to grab his shirt and pull him closer to her. "I missed you." She wrapped her arms around his middle.

He returned the hug. He couldn't help it. He wanted so much to hold her, and this was one of his few opportunities. "I missed you too," he murmured.

"I've only been gone a few hours."

"Well, you said you missed me."

"I've missed you for the past few weeks."

He sighed, a feeling of pleased understanding spreading out through his chest. "I've missed you too," he admitted.

She pressed her cheek against his shirt and squeezed her arms around him. He held her, fighting the almost irresistible impulse to tilt her head up so he could kiss her.

He could probably seduce her tonight. She'd had a little too much to drink. Her resistance was lowered. It probably wouldn't be hard to get her back into his bed, exactly where he wanted her.

But he wasn't going to take advantage of her, and that wasn't what he really wanted anyway. He wanted her heart—not just her body—and there were no shortcuts to that.

"Do you think people can change, Mitchell?" she asked, still wrapped up in his arms.

It felt like his heart stopped beating for a minute. "Yes," he said slowly. "Not always and not easily, but I think it's possible."

"I want to change."

"What do you want to change, baby?"

She didn't answer immediately. "I don't always want to hold on so tightly."

He knew exactly what she was talking about. She was referring back to their previous conversations. She'd lived her life holding on tightly to the edges of her world to keep it all from falling apart. It kept her from taking risks, from making herself vulnerable.

It kept her from giving herself to him—even just for a moment.

Breathless now, he murmured, "Just say the word, baby, and I'll help you let go."

He waited to see if she would say it, but the silence stretched on so long that he knew tonight wasn't the night.

The night might never come, but it was definitely not tonight.

"Thank you," she mumbled, her face now pressed into his shirt.

He kissed the top of her head. "Anytime."

~

"You're kidding!" Rose said, her voice breathless on the phone. "I can't believe the six months are actually over and you guys still haven't managed to get it together."

Deanna sighed over the blackberry crumble she was preparing. "I keep telling you that there's only a small chance of something happening. We are who we are, and we're as different as night and day."

"Yeah, but I think that actually works for you two. And I keep telling you that nothing is going to happen unless you actually say something. He needs to know you want something more."

Deanna's belly twisted with nerves. She'd been thinking it over for the past few weeks, and she'd almost come to a decision about it. Now that her time was up, she had no choice but to act or to give up completely. "I know."

Rose gasped on the other end of the call. "Really? You're going to say something?"

"I think so. We're having dinner tonight—just a quiet dinner for our last evening of the six months—so I thought I'd say something then. I'm just trying to figure out… it's hard, you know. Not just because it's… it's not something I do but because he's been acting so standoffish lately. I'm not sure if he's even interested anymore—even for now, much less forever."

"Of course he's interested. I thought you told him he had to back off."

"I did. I mean, we agreed. But he seems to be getting more standoffish as the weeks go by, so I'm just not sure anymore. Anyway, I think I'd better say something or I'll spend the rest of my life wishing I did."

"That's for sure."

"I'm just trying to think of a way to get him to loosen up again. He hasn't even been acting like himself lately. It's like… I don't know. I almost want him to blow up, just so he'll be himself again."

"So do something to make him mad."

Deanna giggled. "You should have seen how mad he was after we pulled the curtain back to show him the Pride that first day. He was sneezing his head off and totally shocked, but he was so mad when he could finally—" She broke off, suddenly hit with a crazy, brilliant idea.

"What?" Rose asked. "What just happened?"

"I've got an idea. Oh, I don't know if I should do it or not."

"The answer is yes. If you're not sure, then the answer is definitely yet. This is your last chance!"

"Right." Deanna's head was whirling, and her heart was racing in excitement. It was crazy. It was foolish. It was absolutely ridiculous.

But she was definitely going to do it.

Mitchell came home from work a little late, and he was quiet and polite when he finally did. He complimented the food she'd prepared, and he told her she looked very pretty—she'd dressed in a cotton sundress with a little white sweater over it—and he made pleasant conversation about their days and about her grandmother and about his sister and about how his mother was coming up in two weeks to visit the Darlington Café, which was about to reopen under his management.

But it didn't feel at all like him.

She was getting worried since it felt almost like he was going through the motions. Maybe he was now looking forward to being done with their marriage. Maybe all of what she'd sensed in him—depth and feeling and growing determination—had faded away as the weeks passed on.

It didn't matter. She was going to do this. She had no choice now since everything was prepared.

So, when they finished the main course, she said with a smile, "I made dessert. I thought we might eat it in the TV room if that's okay. We could watch a movie or something."

"Sure," he said with a smile. "Sounds good."

She went to the kitchen to get the blackberry crumble and ice cream, and when she carried the two bowls into the other room, she saw he'd lit a few candles and turned on music.

She blinked at him in surprise, although the ambience was very nice.

Just as she was carrying the bowls over to him, he gave a dramatic sneeze.

"Sorry," he said sheepishly. "That was very attractive, wasn't it?"

She giggled, feeling another surge of excitement since it seemed to be on his mind that he wanted to be attractive for her.

"That looks really good," he said, taking one of the bowls. "I suppose you want to eat on the floor, don't you?"

"Sure. If you don't mind."

They lowered themselves to the floor and started to eat. Two bites in, Mitchell sneezed again. And three bites later, he sneezed once more.

"What the hell?" he asked, wiping his nose with a napkin. "You didn't decide to buy a cat or something, did you?"

"Of course not." She kept her eyes wide and her face perfectly composed, but he must have seen something in her expression because he looked at her suspiciously.

"What's going on?" he demanded.

"Nothing. What do you mean?"

"I mean you look—" The words broke off with another sneeze. "What the hell did you do?"

"I didn't do anything. Maybe you should open a window and get some fresh air." She thought she did a really good job of acting innocent, but Mitchell clearly wasn't convinced.

The sneezing was getting out of control though, so he hauled himself to his feet and went to open the blackout shades that covered the windows.

He roared in surprised shock when the shades revealed four members of the Pride perched there on the wide ledge in all their tattered feline glory.

Deanna covered her mouth with her hand and tried not to laugh out loud.

He whirled around and glared at her, but the effect was marred by two more sneezes.

"I thought you might want something to remember me by," she told him, her eyes still wide and innocent, "so I talked Grandmama into sacrificing these four."

"Why…" A sneeze. "Why… why… why…" Another sneeze. He mopped at his face.

"I was kind of hoping you'd get mad at me and act normal again," she admitted.

"What?" His expression had changed, even through the twisting of his allergy attack.

"I wanted you to act more like yourself. All your gentlemanly civility for the past few weeks has been kind of freaking me out. I missed the real Mitchell, so I thought the Pride might help to resurrect him."

He stared at her, his eyes watering helplessly, but something had definitely transformed on his face.

Then, to her surprise, he whirled around and left the room.

Maybe he was really mad. Maybe he hadn't truly understood what she was trying to say, trying to do. Or maybe the allergy was simply too much. It was kind of mean, after all.

She went over to the dead cats, who had fulfilled their strange duty admirably, and was about to box them up and move them out of the house, when Mitchell returned.

He carried a box wrapped up in silver paper.

"What is that?" she asked.

He opened his mouth to answer, but a sneeze came out instead. He just handed the box to her, nodding in its general vicinity.

She understood this meant she should open it, so she did.

Under the paper was a white box, and she lifted the lid to reveal some tissue paper and then something that made her gasp audibly.

It was beaded fabric. All her favorite beads—the ones she'd been collecting but never doing anything with, the ones she's been gathering for years.

She stared down, mesmerized by the textured beauty of the colors and shine.

Finally, she lifted it out and saw it wasn't just a clutch or a bag. It was a wall hanging, exactly as she'd envisioned. A large one, using all the beads.

Her eyes burned as she stared at it, as she realized how incredibly long it must have taken to make it.

"It's not…" He sneezed and wiped at his face. "It's not perfect. You can redo it if you want."

She was choking now on rising emotion. "I'm not going to redo it! You did this for… for me?"

"Of course for you. You said it was too much work just for you to keep it. You thought you weren't worth it. I wanted to show you that you are. I know it's…" He turned away to sneeze a couple of times. "I know it's kind of cheesy, but it was just an idea I had. It's okay if you—"

Deanna burst into tears.

She carefully put the beaded fabric down in the box and then threw herself into Mitchell's arms.

He wrapped his arms around her tightly, but since she was crying and he was sneezing, it wasn't exactly the most romantic of embraces.

"Okay," he said, pulling away, his face flushed and his eyes still watering. "We're going to do it all here in the sight of the Pride since that was what you wanted."

He fumbled until he found her hand, and then he lifted it to hold it in his. He gently pulled off her rings, separating out her engagement ring and then sliding it into his pocket. When he pulled his hand back out, he was holding a different ring instead.

It was beautifully engraved gold with a lovely diamond setting. It looked like an antique—full of history and meaning that spanned generations.

He slid the new ring on her finger with her wedding ring.

"I never should have given you that other ring," he said. "It was wrong. It was empty. It wasn't like you at all." He sniffed and paused, like he would sneeze, but he didn't. "I love you, Deanna Beaufort Graves. I love you with everything I have in me to love—which is so much more than I ever knew before I met you. I don't want to take the easy route with you. I want to do the hardest thing, the most beautiful thing. I want to work as hard as we need to work to get this right. I'll be as patient as you need me to be. I'll wait as long as you need me to wait. But I'm not going to give up on this, because I know it's the right thing for both of us. I think you know it too. I understand why you didn't trust me before, but as soon as you do, I hope you'll let go. I promise I'll be there to catch you when you do."

He broke off with a huge sneeze that jarred both of them.

"Damn it," he muttered. "I almost got through the whole speech."

She burst into laughter and tears at the same time and grabbed him in another hug, this time pressing kisses all over his face. "I love you too. I was going to tell you tonight too after I loosened you up with the Pride. I know there are no guarantees in love, in marriage, in life, in anything. But I want you anyway. I want you all the way. I want you exactly as you are."

Mitchell made a rough sound in his throat and grabbed her face in a deep kiss. She kissed him back, eagerly, her arms wrapping around his neck, until he had to break away to sneeze again.

"Okay," he said. "Either we go or the Pride goes."

"The Pride can go," she said, filled with so much joy she knew it was it spilling out of her somehow. "They've done their job."

"Just don't tell your grandmother. I'll never hear the end of it if she knows that her dead cats had any hand in getting us together."

Deanna giggled. "Too late. She already knows."

EPILOGUE

Deanna fumbled to the door of their bedroom, trying unsuccessfully to open it. Mitchell had her pressed up against the door, kissing her as if his life depended on it.

She was so turned on that it felt like hers might depend on it too.

He'd lifted one of her thighs and was holding it up next to his leg, spreading her open just enough for her to feel the pressure of his body against her arousal. She moaned, still scrabbling to turn the doorknob.

When it finally turned, it surprised her, and she gasped as the door started to open.

It evidently surprised Mitchell too since he briefly lost his balance, and they started to fall backward as the door opened into the room.

He caught them before there was a disaster, dropping her thigh and grabbing her with both arms to stabilize her. Then he was kissing her again, walking them back toward the bed.

He was hard and hot and eager, and nothing had ever felt so good. He was all there—all of him—and all of him was completely into her.

That knowledge affected her as much as the physical sensations, and her body was buzzing with excitement and emotion when the back of her legs hit the edge of the bed and they both tumbled onto it.

He didn't stop kissing her, even as they clumsily started pulling at each other's clothes. He was more successful than she was, and soon she was naked except for her panties. She got held up on his tie, which she accidentally kept tightening instead of loosening.

The third time, he coughed as she started to strangle him and broke out of the kiss. "I'll do it," he said huskily, his eyes hot and soft. "Since I want to survive long enough to get inside you."

She made a face at him, but she was pretty sure it wasn't effective since she was melting with affectionate feelings. As he pulled his tie off, she started working on the buttons on his shirt, and pretty soon they together got his shirt and T-shirt off so his chest was bared.

Running her hands up and down it, she smiled. "Much better."

"Well, don't rest on your laurels too much. We still have work to do." After a pause, he cocked one eyebrow. "I'm still wearing my pants."

She broke into giggles and pulled him down into another kiss. The kiss grew deeper and hotter until desire was filling her head again and she was fumbling with his belt and then the top button on his trousers.

She had better luck with the pants and was soon able to pull them down and then push down his underwear so she could finally get her hands on his erection.

He huffed into her mouth as she stroked him between their bodies. She adjusted so she could wrap both legs around his thighs, and she rocked beneath him, unable to stay still.

"Deanna," he gasped, breaking his mouth out of the kiss and panting against her skin. "Baby, wait."

She tried to rub herself against him. "I don't want to wait."

"But…"

She grabbed his head back down to kiss him again. He moaned into her mouth, not moving against her as rhythmically as usual.

"Mitchell, please," she murmured, tightening her legs around him.

He groaned again and pulled his head away, against the resistance of her hands. His eyes were now torn between desperate desire and amusement. "I'm trapped in my pants."

The words managed to process in her lust-clouded brain, and she peered around his chest so she could see what had happened. His trousers had somehow managed to twist up as she'd pushed them down so they were tightened around his knees like a vice.

She giggled helplessly.

He gave her an aggrieved look. "You're the one who did it."

"I know." She couldn't stop laughing even as she tried to untwist them enough to get them off his legs completely.

"I'm in a pretty bad condition here, you know."

"I know. So am I." She smiled up at him, suddenly filled with so much love she couldn't possibly contain it. "You have no idea how much I love you."

"I love you too. But if you're going to leave me trapped like this, maybe you can at least help me turn over so my dick is accessible."

She was still giggling as she got his pants and underwear off all the way, and then she slid off her own panties and repositioned herself, spreading her legs to make room for him. "There. Now you're all set."

"Oh, good." He was smiling too, as if he was filled with the same feelings that she was. And when he kissed her this time it was almost gentle. As he did, he guided himself inside her body, the penetration tight and pleasing.

They rocked together tenderly for a while, kissing and stroking each other. But eventually the intense need took over and their motion intensified. Soon he was thrusting into her hard and fast, and she was crying out as her orgasm coiled up inside her.

They were so shamelessly enthusiastic that the bed was shaking wildly as her climax finally broke and she arched up with a cry of completion. He was right behind her, muffling his exclamation with another kiss.

They collapsed together afterward, clinging to each other. She loved the feel of his hot, satisfied body on top of her almost more than anything else.

After a few minutes, he lifted his head to gaze down on her. "Well, aside from a few minor issues, that was amazing."

"That was amazing—issues and all."

He stroked her hair gently away from her damp face. "Happy anniversary."

She grinned up at him. "Happy anniversary to you too." Without thinking, she glanced above the bed, where she'd hung the beaded wall-hanging he'd worked so hard on and given her six months ago. Her chest still constricted at the sight—even after so long—of how determined he was to show her just how hard he would work to have her, to keep her.

He'd never let her down.

"Don't get too sappy," he murmured, evidently reading her expression.

She cleared her throat and looked back at him. "Never. You know, I was thinking that we really need to have two anniversaries each year. One for when we got married and another one for when we really came together."

He shook his head. "That seems a sneaky way of getting two anniversary gifts a year."

"Of course. Why else would I suggest it?"

Adjusting her body so she was nestled against him more comfortably, he idly caressed her back and bottom. "I can manage that."

She rested her left hand on his chest, the engagement ring and wedding rings prominent. "Remember, you were supposed to have a wife who was easy to manage. I'm not sure that worked out very well for you."

He leaned up to press a kiss against her hair. "It didn't work out at all. You're impossible to manage. But that ended up working out even better for me, so I'm not about to complain."